Golden Dollar

© Marc Alexander

ISBN 978-1-909473-16-4

Text prepared by www.willowebooks.org.uk

Golden Dollar

by

Marc Alexander

Published by Willow Books

CHAPTER 1

There was a sickening lurch. The ship-like swaying and creaking of the Wells Fargo coach ceased. From outside floated a fluent string of cusswords uttered by the driver. It was cut short by a harsh voice shouting: 'Don't touch your guns, d'ya hear, don't touch your guns!'

'My Gawd, a holdup!' gasped the tubby man opposite, the only other passenger on the Tombstone Stage. His face had gone a sickly clay colour, his baby blue eyes popped and his hand clawed under his frock coat. I thought he was having a heart attack until I realised he was grabbing for his wallet. Perhaps he had some notion of stashing it away somewhere.

'You in there, c'mon out – and don't get any fancy ideas about bein' heroes.'

Obeying the command, I climbed into the eye-searing sunlight. By squinting in the sudden glare I saw the bandit ahead of the coach. His hat was pulled down low and his red bandana covered the bottom half of his face. There was a wet patch on it where it touched his mouth. His Sharps rifle was pointed in our general direction. It was as steady as a rock which indicated that this road agent was no nervous novice. Further up the trail another masked figure sat on a horse, keeping us covered as well.

'Okay, I'm gonna make a collection,' said the masked man, making a move to dismount. 'Shell out – and smile.'

'My Gawd, my Gawd...' muttered the little guy

beside me. Just then the driver's mate decided he ought to earn his pay as a guard. His shotgun was still on the seat beside him. He grabbed it, fumbled...but before he could use it, outlaw No. 2 fired. The crash of his Remington and the scream of the guard chased each other across the plain to the distant hills that made a ragged skyline.

The noise triggered me off. My hand smacked against the butt of my Colt Peacemaker. Next second I had it steadied over my left forearm and was firing fast. At times like this one acts with a sort of instinct. All I knew was I objected to being held up. The gunplay was automatic. My first slug went wide, but as I glanced along the 7½-inch barrel at the red-masked man I just knew my shot would get him in the centre of the chest.

It did – just as the Sharps exploded and woodwork from the coach splintered by my ear. The second bandit was pumping bullets at us now, but making the fatal and common mistake of not taking cool aim. Maybe he was too excited, maybe these two were not used to victims who fought back.

I fired again. The bullet from the Peacemaker hit his horse. The poor critter reared up with a whinny and I fired again. The shot found its mark. The bandit rolled from the saddle. The wounded horse lunged off, dragging its dead master through the scrub by a foot still caught in the stirrup iron.

My fellow traveller, who had been prone on the ground while the lead had been flying, felt called upon to make a remark. He came out with the old platitude: 'God created men, Colonel Colt made them equal...'

'Amen to that,' I heard myself say though, I felt a wave of nausea and guilt at having snuffed out two human lives.

Reason argued it was them or me, but still the sick feeling remained. I guess this was the basic difference between me and a professional gunslinger – the pro feels a great sense of pleasure when he downs someone. I think it was Johnny Ringo who once remarked it was like making love, only ten times better.

The driver was bending over his stricken buddy who was moaning and bleeding fast from the side.

'Must get him to a doc,' said the driver. 'Lift him inside, fellas.' We laid the guard across the back seat and I pressed my kerchief over the wound. The driver lashed his team until the coach was swaying along the trail as though all the Apaches in Arizona were after it.

'That was mighty fine shooting, sir,' my companion said, still clutching his wallet. 'May I enquire your name?'

'Surely. I'm Bill Tashlin,' I replied. Almost as I expected, he gave a whistle.

'The Bill Tashlin. Well, well, there'll be some good copy for me in this,' and he tugged out a very large notebook.

'I must explain, sir,' he continued. 'I am Milton Homer, a humble though industrious newspaper reporter employed by Mr Clum on his recently established Tombstone Epitaph. So you see I know about you, Mr Tashlin, and your skill with a handgun. But are you aware that Joshua Noon is in Tombstone?'

As he said it he looked eagerly into my face as though he expected me to burst into tears or something. Joshua Noon was the fastest gunman from Yuma to El Paso. I had never seen him, but I had heard enough to know he was a professional entirely devoted to the deadly ironmongery he carried strapped to his thigh.

Such a professional is just about the loneliest guy in the whole world. He has to be dedicated to his ruthless calling just as a priest is devoted to his vocation. He dare not drink like other men in case the liquor slows his reflexes. He must live alone, an invisible wall of fear surrounding him. Like a violinist, he must practise every day with his particular instrument because he knows sooner or later he is going to meet another a professional like himself, only maybe a bit faster on the draw.

Because of this the real top guns keep out of each other's way most of the time. They know it is a good bet that if two of them meet up one will be dead before long. Their reputations mean a lot to them.

Nearly all such men as Joshua Noon are wanderers, living on their fame from town to town, working their own particular 'circuit' like travelling showmen. Often some kid, eager to make a tough reputation for himself, is tempted to pick a fight with a professional gunslinger. Then there is another notch on a sixgun butt, or occasionally a dead gunman and a kid setting out in his victim's footsteps.

I mention all this because it explains Mr Milton Homer's excitement. There would be two men in Tombstone with gun-fighting reputations, and, one way or another, he could see himself writing a sensational piece for his paper.

'If this is your first visit to Tombstone, Mr Tashlin,' he said, 'permit me to show you round.'

'I'd appreciate that,' I said, 'but out of fairness I must tell you that I have no interest at all in Joshua Noon. I have made this journey for the purpose of seeing a lady.'

The driver's rawhide cracked over the lathered backs of his team and the stage rocked crazily through the shimmering afternoon. The guard moaned in delirium and Milton Homer tried to write things in his notebook.

* * *

Glancing out of the coach window I could see we were rolling into Tombstone. The paint on the one and two storey buildings looked pretty new because Tombstone was a pretty new town. It wasn't so long ago – in 1877 – that Ed Schieffelin came here to prospect.

Then there had been nothing but desert and

4

Apaches. In fact, when Ed had told an army officer he was going to try his luck in this barren part of the world, the officer remarked: 'All you'll find will be your tombstone.' That nearly happened. A war party actually trailed Ed's footprints through the sand while he watched them from atop a hillock where he had sheltered for the night.

After he had given the Apaches the slip, he discovered the silver ore which gave him one of the richest mines in the country. Remembering the warning, he ironically called his mine The Tombstone. The name became that of the town which grew up around the great silver lode.

The coach juddered to a halt at the Wells Fargo office on Fifth Street. We carried the unconscious guard inside and a stable lad was sent running for the doctor. There was nothing else we could do, so I collected my grip and followed Milton Homer to the San Jose Rooming House which stood on the corner of Fifth and Fremont Streets.

'I'm sure you'll find it comfortable here, Mr Tashlin,' he said as he led me in. 'There's a room vacant next to mine.' There was no doubt that I was going to have the reporter around me for as long as I was going to be in town. I did not mind as I might find him useful in my quest here.

'Not many people about,' he said to the desk clerk.

'They're buryin' Margarita up at Boothill,' explained the clerk, cutting himself a wad of black tobacco.

'Come with me, Mr Tashlin,' said Milton. 'It should be an inspiring burying, and I must take some notes on the preacher's remarks...' I was going to refuse when the clerk said: 'This Margarita was Joshua Noon's gal until he took an interest in Golden Dollar. The two girls had a fight...an' Golden Dollar won.' I pricked up my ears. I had come a long way to see a dancehall girl called

5

Golden Dollar.

'I'll come,' I told Milton. We set out in the late afternoon sun for Boothill which is just a short way out of town.

It is so called because very few of its customers died through natural causes. Tombstone has the original Boothill graveyard, but the name was so appropriate that dozens of towns in the West have their own Boothills now.

We reached it and joined a large crowd of spectators just as the headboard was being put in place. It was a very simple one, saying:

Margarita stabbed by Gold Dollar.

'I thought her name was Golden Dollar,' I said to Milton.

'That's what they call her,' he replied. 'But Luke Sawyer is a drunken old cuss and after he'd painted GOLD he finished off the Red Eye he'd been given to do the job. Then he carried on with the next word. I guess nobody's going to complain, though. He got the rest right.'

The hot evening wind rattled the spikey crucifixion thorn that grew round the graves. As the preacher began his address I looked at some of the other headboards.

Quite a few had one word 'Unknown' painted on them. Others had a name with a laconic 'Hanged' after it. Some had 'Killed by Indians' as epitaphs. Most had the name of the victim and the party responsible for putting them underground. This meant that several living citizens of Tombstone had their names on headboards in Boothill. I wondered how Golden Dollar felt about having her name over Margarita's grave. I was wondering pretty hard about Golden Dollar!

Only one epitaph had any claim to literary merit. It read:

Here lies Lester Moore Four slugs from a .44 No

6

Less, no more.

Milton saw me looking at it and whispered that Lester had been a Wells Fargo agent who had been shot down by a thief. I reflected – after the events of the afternoon – that there must be safer occupations than working for Wells Fargo.

The preacher was getting pretty worked up over Margarita by now. Standing by the fresh grave, he thundered: 'An' we must think, brothers, of what the good Lord will say when Margarita gets to the top of them Golden Stairs...' (Over Milton's shoulder I saw him scribble 'golden stairs' in his big notebook.)

'What will the good Lord say to this poor sinful gal...?' demanded the preacher.

'Sister, you have took the wrong direction,' yelled someone. There was a chuckle all round. Nothing like a burying to give the simple citizens of Tombstone a chance to sharpen up their wit.

'The Lord will say "Thou is a sinful dancehall gal, Margarita, who was no better than you should be – as many a sinner in this wicked town can testify – but in my mercy I shall open up the great Golden Gates and wash away your sins and make you welcome... which is more than I'll do when that goddam Golden Dollar faces her day of judgement. For such varmints as her there is nothing but hellfire, brimstone and the torment of the deepest pit of Satan's Kingdom." 'And so he went on, thoroughly enjoying himself while Milton wrote down such words as 'hellfire', 'doom', and 'damnation'.

Sometimes, when the preacher paused for breath, some of the spectators would let rip a 'Hallelujah!' just to let him know that his performance was appreciated. All around, it was considered one of the best Boothill buryings for months, and when we got back to town – just as the sun was slipping behind the distant purple hills – everyone had worked up a pretty good thirst.

7

CHAPTER 2

It was evening when I strolled into the Crystal Palace saloon. It stood next door to the office of the Tombstone Epitaph where, no doubt, a compositor was setting up Milton Homer's vivid prose on the subject of the deceased Margarita.

The Saloon was well named. Light sparkled from the chandeliers and glittered in the fancy work of the mirrors. I walked up to the handsome bar and ordered a beer, Milton sidled up to the bar after me.

As I had entered the batwing doors a strange hush had fallen on the assembly, a hush not unfamiliar to me. It was the stillness that follows the entry of a known gunman into a saloon. It was caused by a tensing of the muscles, a certain watchfulness, a certain fear and, above all, a certain excitement. I had first got to know it when I shot a man down just before my twentieth birthday.

It was obvious that Milton had spread the good word and the clientele of the Crystal Palace had no doubt that William Tashlin, Colt expert, was among their number. No doubt what made this particular hush extra pregnant was the fact that at the faro table at the far end of the room sat a figure dressed in black – the famous Joshua Noon.

'I sure hope there ain't gonna be trouble, Mr Tashlin,' muttered the bar-keep as he slid the beer towards me. 'There ain't been a shootin' here for weeks and I've kinda got used to the peace.'

'Don't worry,' I said. 'I ain't looking for trouble.

The problem is...' and here I raised my voice as loudly as possible, '...that when a man gets a reputation like Mr Noon or myself trouble comes sorta unexpected.'

With my drink in my hand I turned and faced the saloon. I wanted to get a good look at the man in black. At first glance you might not have thought he was a top gun. He wore a frock coat, like a lawyer, and a curly brimmed derby. His hands were white and soft, like a woman's. The only hint of colour about him was the glitter of a gold watch chain across his silk waistcoat and the glint of ice blue under his pale eyebrows.

Carefully he placed his glass of mineral water on the edge of the faro table and said: 'Welcome, Mr Tashlin. I hear tell you did some fancy shootin' this afternoon.'

'I believe you're a good judge of shootin', Mr Noon,' I replied. He should be – it was rumoured he had won seventeen duels! I noticed he had brushed back the flap of his coat so that he could easily reach the ivory butt of his Navy Colt with the filed-down foresight.

'Are you aiming to stay or are you just passin' through?' he asked politely.

'I'm just passin' through,' I answered with equal courtesy. 'I just expect to spend a few peaceful days here and then be on my way.'

'Let's get on with the game, then,' Noon said, turning to the other players.

A sigh seemed to go up. You could almost hear the nerves relaxing all round now it was plain Noon and I weren't out to slaughter each other.

Maybe it was this anticlimax that made Noon feel the need to get tough. He sipped his mineral water, then looked at me coldly. 'You say you want it peaceful, Mr Tashlin. If you really do, I suggest you use the Oriental Saloon. It's on the other corner...'

'I drink where I please, Mr Noon,' I replied. 'Who knows, I may prefer the company there.' With that remark

9

I downed my beer and walked into Allen Street. It did not worry me if it seemed the gunman had driven me off. I had come some hundreds of miles for something more important than bandying wisecracks with a professional killer.

Outside in the velvet night Milton Homer materialised beside me.

'Where do I find Golden Dollar?' I asked.

He whistled. 'Joshua Noon is very interested in that young lady right now,' he said.

'I'd still like to know where I can find her.'

'She's a dancer at the Birdcage. Come with me, Mr Tashlin.'

We walked along a block in the direction of some gay music, passing Jacob Meyer's Clothing Store from whose shadows assassins had shot down Virgil Earp not so long ago.

The Birdcage Theatre came as a surprise. As Milton and I entered we were dazzled by the light that illuminated the stage and reflected from mirrors and gilt. The seats were covered with red plush, and each side of the stage there were proper boxes like theatres have in the East. It was full of miners whooping it up. Waiters dashed about with trays of drinks while on the stage a man in a top hat was singing *Buffalo Gals*, and a line of girls did a high-spirited dance in the background.

I have seen many such places of entertainment in my travels, but the Birdcage was one of the best. It was a proper music hall and a tribute to the money that was being made from the booming Tombstone silver mines.

Milton pointed to a bearded, unkempt man sitting alone in one of the boxes.

'A mad Russian,' he whispered. 'Been in Tombstone nigh on a year and sits in that box every night. They say he's crazy on one of the girls who work the circuit, and he keeps hoping she'll appear here again.

Trouble is he can't speak English or I could write him up... maybe something like "Nephew of the Czar Seeks Wandering Showgirl – Who is the Modern Cinderella?" '

I could not help laughing at the reporter. His only interest in life seemed to be in translating it into columns of print. I'd bet the greatest token of his friendship he could offer would be to write up my obituary in his purple prose.

The gent in the top hat sang some more songs. The girls behind him showed as much leg as possible. The miners kept the waiters running. Then the band struck a chord and the master of ceremonies said, 'Gentlemen, for your especial entertainment, Golden Dollar!'

There were a few boos and a lot of cheers. The Russian in the box bit his nails and looked sad. Then on to the stage came the girl I had come so far to find. She was certainly something to look at, blonde hair down to her shoulders – golden, in fact; and a supple, exciting figure that her tight velvet gown did nothing to hide. But behind her professional manner, behind her tight smile and makeup, I could see her face was white and drawn. Maybe she was not used to stabbing people.

She missed the note, but when the band started for the second time she seemed to have got control of her nerves and sang a song about being a bird in a gilded cage. Several others in a similar sad vein followed. But if the songs were sad, they did not sadden the audience. Golden Dollar was the sort of girl they didn't see often, and they were making the most of it. Several drunks had to be restrained by force frorh climbing on to the stage.

'A fine looking gal,' pronounced Milton, throwing a crafty look into my face. 'No wonder Joshua Noon has taken a fancy to her. You'll see more of her, she does a dance number as well.'

He was right. Later in the programme she came on in a costume that seemed to be made entirely of feathers.

11

She sang a bit, then did a dance routine while a line of girls high-kicked in the background.

I had no reason to like her. In fact, I had some good reasons to feel the opposite way about her. Yes, I must admit there was something about this girl they called Golden Dollar that made my pulses pound a little faster. Maybe too much time had gone by since I last looked closely at an attractive girl.

It was just after midnight when the show came to an end. While the waiters were busy chucking out the drunks, I followed Milton to the back of the theatre.

'I wanna see Golden Dollar,' I told a wizen little guy who guarded the stage door. I crossed his palm with silver.

'No trouble, pal,' he croaked.

'Room No. 1. She's the main attraction now that Margarita...ahem...'

With Milton beside me I knocked on the door of the main dressing-room. (Getting rid of Milton when he smelt a story would be like trying to lose your shadow.)

'Yeah?' came Golden Dollar's voice.

'May I come in. I'd like to have a few words...'

'I'll bet. Run off, fella, whoever you are.'

'Are you Louisa Sherman...?' I hollered through the door.

There was a silence, then the click of a lock being undone and I entered. Golden Dollar, now in a dressing-gown, went back to the mirror and continued to clean off her makeup.

I was surprised that close up she looked as good as she did on the stage. As yet the dry Arizona air had not spoiled her skin, nor had the late hours and the inevitable whisky bottle put dark rings under her eyes.

'What was that name you mentioned, mister?' she asked.

'Louisa Sherman,' I said. 'I've been looking for

12

Louisa Sherman for months. I've even used the Pinkertons. In fact it was one of their agents who spotted you here and sent me the good word.'

'You'd better sit down. You've got a lot of explaining to do, mister.' She spoke coldly and arrogantly, and I knew I was going to dislike her more than I had expected.

But I sat. Milton sat behind me. I wondered if his notebook was out yet.

'Now tell me, mister – why the hell should you check up on me?'

'If I tell you my name is Tashlin, Bill Tashlin, would that explain anything?'

Her eyes narrowed.

' Keep talking, mister.'

'Okay,' I said, trying to control an anger that I felt growing inside me. It was an old anger that I felt every time my mind strayed back to the reason of my search.

'My old man was called Bill Tashlin, too. He and your father were partners five years back.'

'What is that to me? I was back East then. I know nothing of my father's business. He died over two years ago.'

'Let me tell you about it. For a long time our fathers had been prospecting together. They never had much luck, but my old man always had a hunch there was gold somewhere along the Gila River. About six years ago they struck out with three Mexicans and a team of mules...and disappeared. Only your father returned.'

'I heard about that. The Indians...'

'Apparently they did find gold,' I continued, ignoring the interruption. 'I guess they got more than they ever dreamed of. Rather than start a rush, they stayed out in the wilderness for nearly twelve months until they had so much their mules could hardly carry it. Then they started back across the Gila Desert.

13

'Now, according to Sherman's – your father's – story, they had been travelling slowly when they were overtaken by Apaches under Red Cloud. According to his same story, my father and the three Mexicans were killed, but your father managed to escape without the gold. He finally reached Yuma more dead than alive.'

'Like I said, I was back East at the time,' Golden Dollar said calmly, 'but I did hear about it. So what, Mr Tashlin?'

'So this, Miss Sherman never believed that goddam story. It stinks like a dead steer. My old man was the son of one of the first traders ever to come to this territory. He grew up with the Indians before the troubles. What your father didn't know when he concocted the story was something few people know, namely that Red Cloud and my father used to play together as kids. They were blood brothers, and Red Cloud would have taken his own life before he would have hurt a hair on my Dad's head. My family has always been friends with Apaches.'

'The fact remains that your father did not come back and the gold was lost,' said Golden Dollar. But this time she was not looking me insolently in the face as before.

'Sure,' I said. 'But when the news finally reached me, I figured a few things out. My old man must have struck it very rich to stay out there so long. My father, your father and their Mexican companions must have been coming back pretty rich men. Still, it is better to have the whole lot rather than just a share. At least, that's what some men think. And from what I was able to find out, it's the sort of thing your father would have figured. He's been mixed up in plenty of wickedness in his time. My bet is he shot down his mates and then hid the gold.'

I expected her to leap at me, to claw my face. Anyone would if their father had just been called a murderer. But Golden Dollar just started brushing her hair. The only thing was that her eyes had begun to glitter like blue diamonds.

'If this story you have just told me is true, Mr Tashlin, and you must believe it seeing you have spent a lot of effort to come and tell it to me...what has it got to do with me? I have not seen my father since I was twelve years old. Whatever he did, it has nothing to do with me. Will you please go now.'

'Not yet, Golden Dollar,' I snapped. 'Somewhere out in the desert there is a treasure of gold. My old man found it, and died for it – and I mean to get it. I know your father died two years later. He died a poor and sick man in the Tucson jail, but I'll bet his secret never died with him. He sent a letter East just before he died, and I'll bet he told you his secret in it.'

Golden Dollar laid down her hair brush. Calmly she opened her dressing gown and I heard Milton Homer's breath whistle slightly at the sight of her silk-stockinged leg. With a deft movement she pulled something from the dark red band of her garter. It was a tiny .41 Colt Derringer. With her right hand she pointed it straight at my abdomen while she used her other to rearrange her robe.

'Out, Mr Tashlin,' she hissed in a voice that would have been like the voice of a snake, supposing a snake could speak. 'Your story is a dirty lie. Go before I give you what you deserve, you gun-slinging bully...'

'Like father, like daughter,' I remarked bitterly. 'But I am interested you can use a gun as well as a knife. Do you reserve the knife for your own sex?'

In the circumstances, that remark could have cost me dearly, but it had an unexpected effect. Her face seemed as though it was about to crumple. 'That was self defence,' she whispered. I laughed harshly as I stood up and backed away.

'And what about you!' she suddenly snarled,

15

getting mad again. 'You're a great gun expert, too. Oh yes, I've heard of you, Bill Tashlin. I believe your last victim was only sixteen.'

By now she was shaking so much with rage that I knew I was in real danger. I shot out of the door, which had been thoughtfully opened by Milton. It slammed in our faces.

'Whew!' he whistled as we went into the cold star-scattered night. 'There's sure a story in that.'

'Milton,' I said, 'if you write one word about this it will be the last word you write this side of paradise. But if you wait until it's all over, if you give me your word as – as – as a gentleman of the Press, then I'll give you enough material to write a book.'

'It's a deal,' he said, pumping my hand and I could almost feel him beaming in the dark.

As we walked away from the now silent Birdcage I noticed a still figure watching us from the main doorway. He sucked on his cigarette, and in the brief glow I recognised the cruel face of Joshua Noon.

CHAPTER 3

It was early next morning when I strolled through the streets of Tombstone. The only signs of life were thin smoke lines that pencilled straight up from the chimneys of the wooden buildings.

Out at the mines the diggers were probably covered in sweat as they struggled to extract yet more silver ore, but here the town was still sleeping off the effects of the night before.

I liked it this way. I needed to think. Almost unconsciously I walked down Fremont Street and headed in the direction of Boothill. I was not happy with myself. For the past months I had been so busy tracking down Louisa Sherman, now known as the Golden Dollar, that I had hardly given any thought to what I would do when I finally found her. I guess I had figured I would get her to give me the secret, then I'd find my father's hidden gold... and live happily ever after.

But it was not going to be as easy as that. The dance-hall girl was Sherman's daughter all right, complete with this mean, murderous streak. And then there was the complication of Joshua Noon, that gun-skilled wolf in black. I wondered if she had told him about her father's last letter.

In my mind I was positive that Sherman, when he realised he was dying, had written to her in Philadelphia where she was supposed to be studying to go on the stage. When a man knows his hours are numbered, even a villain like Sherman, he thinks of those he is going to leave behind. If he couldn't take it with him, Sherman would at least want his kin to get it. I had talked to the sheriff of Tucson who was with him when he was dying. He told me that Sherman had struggled to write a letter which he had begged the sheriff to send to his daughter.

My investigations, or rather those of the Pinkerton Agency, showed that soon after she must have got it she gave up her studies and disappeared vaguely west. It could only point to one thing – she must have an idea of the whereabouts of the gold. Then why hadn't she got it? Of course, a girl could not go hunting for it alone in the Apache-infested no-man's-land that stretched between here and the Pacific. She would certainly need a man. Could that man be Joshua Noon? No doubt he was the sort who would attract her.

These thoughts were all mixed up in my head as I ambled along in the early sun. As yet it was still pleasantly cool, though in an hour the landscape would be shimmering with waves of heat-tortured air. Suddenly I remembered her parting remark, the remark about me killing a sixteen-year-old. Even now I winced at it. It was all the worse because it was technically true.

I was a gunslinger all right. I was fast with my Peacemaker and – more important – I was accurate. Like Joshua Noon, I was one of the lonely band of men who were feared by their fellows as though the Mark of Cain glowed on their foreheads. Yet I was a gunman by accident, or so I always told myself. And it had been an accident over that kid!

It had been in a bar at Las Cruces. I had known there was going to be trouble as soon as he swaggered into the saloon. He was a youngster out to make a big reputation for himself. What better short cut to fame than by shooting down Bill Tashlin!

All through the afternoon he eyed me, making sarcastic remarks about me to his bunch of young hangers-on. He was spoiling for a showdown and I knew it had to come as surely as night must follow day.

I could almost smell death about him – his or mine – as he stood at one end of the bar and I lounged at the other. At last he began pitching his remarks so high I could no longer pretend not to hear them.

'He don't look much to me,' he said. 'I kinda figure he looked more like a hoss thief than a gunman. Maybe if you count the guys he plugged in the back, then he might rate as a gunman...'

He had a sixgun strapped to each hip, with a thong round the thigh to hold the holsters flat when he drew. This was just plain showing off. Since Colts no longer needed to be primed, the practice of carrying two guns had died out. Originally the idea of having a couple was to give you a spare in case one did not fire, but the advent of the Thuer revolver cartridge after the Civil War made this unnecessary.

As the kid carried on his stream of abuse I knew I must leave. But as I walked past his group he threw his drink in my face.

'What's the hurry, hoss thief?' he said, and went for his guns.

He actually fired one shot before I got the Peacemaker out, but he was so excited it went wild. I had to get him before he could fire again. And I did.

There was no time to aim so I'd just injure him and, anyway, an injured man can still shoot. So I just fired by instinct and he crumpled. His pals ran off, leaving me and the barkeep looking down at him on the blood spotted floor. There was a look of bewilderment on his face.

It had been him or me. But I hated the memory of that hot afternoon in that mean little bar.

Now I tried to think of my future plans rather than the past. Soon I found myself at the burial ground. The grave markers reflected the increasing glare. By one I saw the figure of a burly man. He was kneeling down at a

19

grave, but he lumbered to his feet as soon as he saw me and plodded away.

It was the Russian Milton Homer had pointed out to me the night before at the Birdcage Theatre. I saw he had left a small posy of desert flowers on Margarita's grave. Well, it was nice that someone mourned her, even if it was only a crazy foreigner whom no one could understand.

I found a patch of shade under a greasewood tree and sat down for a smoke. As I thought again about my problem, the more I became convinced Joshua Noon must be mixed up in this business. Maybe this was why he'd suddenly lost interest in Margarita and taken up with Golden Dollar.

Suddenly a shadow fell across me. I was so startled I was half-way to drawing my gun when I recognised Milton Homer perspiring above me.

'Good morning, Mr Tashlin,' he said. 'A burial plot is a good place for reflective thought, is it not? Only ghosts to disturb you, eh?' Chuckling at his little joke he sat beside me.

'This evening they'll be burying the guard who was shot with us at the holdup yesterday,' he said. 'Poor fellow departed this life during the night.'

This is a dangerous land, Milton,' I said.

'Amen to that,' he responded mechanically. 'In the midst of life...By the way, Joshua Noon has been asking questions about you. I got the notion he's hoping you'll be riding out soon.'

'Oh yes?'

'I think he has enough on his mind without worrying about a rival at arms. I heard a rumour he's waiting here for his old gang who are coming to meet him from across the border...'

'You mean, he's getting his old bunch together again?'

'Yes. He has been in recent telegraphic communication with Nogales.

That's where his gang hid up after their last spot of trouble.'

I rolled another cigarette carefully.

'I think I'm going to leave town after all,' I said. 'I'll take the advice Joshua Noon gave me in the Crystal Palace.'

The reporter's face became long with disappointment. 'But what about...?'

'Listen, Milton, I'm chasing something pretty big. There's a lot at stake, and if you care to help me there'd be a few hundred bucks in it for you.'

'As long as I get the story,' he replied. 'Not that I'm refusing the bucks, mind!'

'You'll get the story,' I grinned. 'It seems to me that Joshua Noon is mixed up in some way with Golden Dollar over my Dad's gold. Now, while I'm around he's gonna be mighty suspicious, especially after she tells him about our meetin' last night. So, I'll pretend to go off. But I'll really only camp a few miles out of town. You could maybe keep an eye on things and let me know what develops. Is that a deal?'

'Sure, it's a deal, Mr Tashlin. I know a good spot not too far out where you'll be reasonably safe, unless a war party finds you. I've heard the Apaches are putting on the paint.'

'Guess I'll have to chance that. I'll hint that I've dropped the idea of gettin' information from Golden Dollar. I'll make out I'm gonna carry on lookin' for the gold on my own.'

We discussed the plan and then walked back to the town. As we walked up Toughnut Street I noticed the loafers under the verandas were watching us with strange curiosity. Milton began to squirm.

'I just remembered a proof I had to correct,' he

blurted out suddenly and disappeared to the office of the *Tombstone Epitaph*.

Something odd was in the air and I was pretty sure Joshua Noon was behind it. Suddenly a kid ran up to me, his face bright pink with self importance.

'Mr Tashlin, Mr Noon says he'd like to see you in the Crystal Palace.' I tossed him a dime and went towards the saloon, and I could feel the eyes of the loafers swivel after me.

After the glare of the Arizona sun, the interior of the saloon seemed as dark and as cool as a cave under the sea. I had to blink several times before I could see properly.

Then I saw Joshua Noon seated alone at a table, a mineral water by his hand. As I approached him I noticed out of the corner of my eye that the bartender and the few early customers had discreetly moved out of the line of fire. Maybe they were expecting a showdown. Well, they were going to be disappointed.

'Mornin',' I said sociably. 'You have words to say?'

'I surely do, Tashlin,' he responded with a smile that would have suited a rattler. 'They're brief. Last night I understand you were hanging around the Birdcage. Well, a certain lady there is a personal friend of mine and I don't like her bein' bothered. Unless you wanna make somethin' of it, my friend, I suggest you leave this town very fast.'

A stray sunbeam winked on his gold watch chain. His white, cared-for hands lay on the table in front of him. He was relaxed, and ready to kill. I wondered if it came to the draw which one of us would survive. He was probably faster than I, but, with his filed foresight, less accurate. It was an interesting question, but not one that I was going to put to the test.

I stood there dumb. The seconds seemed to stretch

into eternity. I did not want to appear to give in too easily, but at the same time I did not want to provoke him. I had to play it very carefully.

Calmly he lifted his mineral water in his left hand. 'I'm gonna start countin', Tashlin,' he drawled. A muscle twitched under his left eye. He was getting the thrill a gunman feels a few seconds before he goes into action, the heady, sick elation that is some sort of perversion. 'If you're not on your way by the time I get to ten, then you'll be the next customer for Boothill. One... two... three...'

I decided to hold my ground until 'seven', then pretended to crack. I shuffled my foot and muttered, 'Okay, okay,' and walked out. Behind me there was a roar of laughter. Joshua Noon had triumphed.

I went to my room, paid the clerk and took my gear to the OK Corral where I quickly bought a likely looking horse. A small group of boys and old loafers followed me, not saying anything but enjoying my humiliation. The groom took my money without a word, having charged me twice what the horse was worth. I swung into the saddle and rode down Allen Street in the direction of the Bisbee trail. One of the kids threw a stone. It hit the horse on the flank and made it rear. There was muffled laughter. I patted its neck and rode on without turning round. As a gunman, I guess my reputation was washed up.

From an upstairs verandah I saw Golden Dollar watching me with a curious expression on her face.

'Coward!' she sneered as I rode past.

That was too much for me. Even though I knew I was only playing the role her one word described, it stuck in my throat. I felt a hot wave of anger rising so I kicked the horse and cantered out of Tombstone.

In my mind it seemed the whole town was laughing now, an infection of mirth inspired by my yellow streak that had spread from the Crystal Palace to the other saloons, through the stores and along the sidewalks. It seemed to pulse mockingly in my ears.

Once past the diggings, I followed the Bisbee trail until I recognised a rock formation Milton had described to me. I turned left and followed a javelina, or wild pig, track which led me through groves of saguaros, those strange cacti which tower up to eighty feet and often live for a couple of centuries or more. I like them. They remind me of petrified giants my mother used to tell me stories about when I was a kid playing round Dad's trading post. The saguaros were the real inhabitants of the desert. My horse and I were intruders.

I rode on for nearly an hour through the heat of noon, then I settled down to camp in a small dry gulch. I picketed the horse, spread out my bedding roll in the shade of a rock and lay down to wait. I took the precautions of having my Winchester by me.

For hours I watched the lizards chasing each other. Then the sun went down and I slept soundly.

It was on the second evening that Milton Homer visited me. The sky was changing from blood red to violet, and the chill of the approaching desert night had made me put on my poncho, when he rode up on his mule with two very welcome waterbags.

'Howdy.' I said, seizing the water-bags and drinking greedily. 'I thought you were going to let me die of thirst. What's been happening in town?'

'Well, I'm afraid they believe you're yellow back there,' he chuckled. 'Three of Joshua Noon's boys have arrived from Nogales, but I heard tell some more are to come. He's surely up to something but no one knows what. It's making the town nervous.'

We talked for a while, then he said: 'I must go back. The paper is going to press and I don't trust those compositors to correct my galleys properly. I'll come out again at sundown as soon as I can.'

24

I gave him a folded fifty, just to make sure of his enthusiasm for the job. Then he rode off and I was left with the coyotes which sometimes howled to each other across the mesquite and sage.

CHAPTER 4

Another day passed with agonising slowness. I lay and sweated it through, wondering if I had been loco to try this plan. Twice, for something to do, I read last week's issue of the *Tombstone Epitaph* which Milton had left behind. When I could get no more out of it, I smoothed out the sand and played cards with myself until the heat of the sun made the pasteboards curl.

It was a relief when it was sundown and a breath of air sighed across the desert. Laying on my back I watched the stars come out, then I cooked a can of beans over a tiny shielded fire. I had to wait until nightfall to do it so the smoke would not show rising above the gulch. I had hoped that Milton would come out with some news, but he did not appear. So I rolled myself up in my blankets and went to sleep.

A slight sound woke me. Without moving my body, I opened my eyes. A bright desert moon illuminated part of the gulch and threw the rest into deep shadow. Someone was coming along it towards me. Carefully I inched the Peacemaker from under the rolled-up poncho which served as a pillow.

Any second now the prowler would appear, right in my pistol sights. I was sure it was not Milton. He would have approached more openly and whistled an agreed signal. Anyone else I could regard as an enemy.

This was a dangerous land.

It was the sudden gleam of gold that eased my finger on the trigger when the dark shape came into view. A cascade of rich blonde hair caught the vivid light of the moon and told me that my visitor was Golden Dollar.

'Stay where you are, I've got you covered,' I hissed. I heard her stifle a cry of fright.

'Mr Tashlin?' she called softly, unable to see me in the shadow.

'It's me all right,' I replied. 'Are you alone?'

'Yes. I want to talk to you.'

'Right. Sit down there in that patch of moonlight. Any tricks an' I'll shoot as happily as if it were your father sitting there.'

'This is no time for feuds,' she said impatiently as she sat down. 'I've come to talk business.'

'First, how did you know where to find me?'

'Milton Homer told me. It has taken me hours...'

'Damn Milton Homer to hell,' I exploded. 'How did he know Joshua Noon and his outfit wouldn't come along as well.!.'

'He knew all right,' she said with a touch of weariness in her voice.

'Joshua Noon and his gang quit Tombstone today. He's double-crossed me...'

'Okay. Let's hear your story from the beginning,' I said, still watching her over my gun barrel. I would have trusted the daughter of Sherman just as I would a rattler.

'You were right in many of the things you said at the Birdcage the other night,' she began, still speaking softly. Somehow one always seems to whisper in the desert.

'My father and yours did strike it rich somewhere out along the Gila,' she continued. 'They mined for nearly a year, then they started back. By then they must have had three mules, the others died of sickness. But those three were loaded with gold. Well, on the way back... something happened...'

'Yes?' I said.

'I'm...I'm not sure about it...I only know anything

27

from a letter my father sent when he was dying. It was a crazy letter, partly in English, partly in Spanish. He must have been delirious some of the time he was writing it because it just did not make sense...'

'Especially the bit about something happening on the way back,' I cut in icily.

She shrugged. 'He never mentioned what happened. But he did say that after what he called "the trouble" he managed to hide a lot of the gold.'

'Did he say where?'

'He did give strange instructions for finding it, but no real names of places that I have been able to find. Perhaps he didn't know the names of the places himself. Anyway, I was studying stage work in Philadelphia when I got the letter finally. It had taken a long time to reach me.

'I decided to find my father's treasure because...well, it was natural that I should want it. So I came West. At first I thought it would be easy, but nowhere could I get a clue. When I found my money had gone, I began working the saloons. I went from town to town, each being one that I knew my father had visited when he was alive. I tried to find out all I could about him, to try and work out where he would have hidden the gold.

'I knew they had found it somewhere along the Gila River, but which way were they going when whatever it was happened? The letter did not say. And I was afraid of showing it to people in case they took advantage of it, just as I was afraid you'd cheat me out of my share when you turned up.'

'Your share!' I exclaimed with a sneer. She ignored it.

Then one day, the girl I was sharing a room with saw the letter...'

'Margarita?'

'Yes. I stupidly told her all about it. Well, she told

her man friend, Joshua Noon. He immediately dropped her and began paying attention to me. At first I did not understand why, though in my so-called profession you get pretty accustomed to men getting a crush on you. But he was different. He hung around all the time, and that was not pleasant. There is a cold, terrifying quality about him. Then, just before you arrived in town, Margarita got drunk and accused me of taking her man. It was terrible. She pulled out a knife. I tried to take it from her, but she fought like a puma. We fell on the floor. She tried to push the tip of the blade into my throat, but I was stronger than she. I bent her wrist back. She struggled more...and somehow it went into her chest. I – I could not believe how easily it went in...and she...she...'

There was silence. She was upset all right. The moonlight glinted on tears running down her cheeks. Yet I was not sure that I believed her story, that this was the way it had been. After all, she was Sherman's daughter and I believe a killer streak can be handed on from one generation to another.

'Go on,' I said at last.

'Well, that's how it happened,' she said simply.

'After that?'

'Joshua Noon hung around. He tried to play a sweet line, but I wasn't interested. Then he came out with it. He wanted the letter Margarita had told him about. He said I would get a share, but I laughed in his face. Then you came along, and you know what happened. I had no more reason to trust you than Joshua Noon. Both of you are gunmen. All I wanted was to be left alone. Then, this afternoon, when I went to my room I found it had been ransacked. Everything was scattered about. All my papers were gone, including that letter.'

'You left it lying about in your room?' I cried, amazed at the stupidity of women.

'It was locked in my trunk, only they smashed the

29

locks. Then I heard that Noon and his gang had ridden out in range clothes and with pack mules.'

'You have a copy of the letter?'

'No. I never thought of it.'

I groaned. 'So what happened after that?'

'I realised you were the only one who could help. I went to see Milton Homer because he'd heard the story in my dressing-room and he might know where you'd gone. I explained everything to him. He brought me most of the way. Now he's waiting down the trail with his mule, ready to give warning if we've been followed. I think he was rather frightened.'

For a moment I grinned, imagining the representative of the Press waiting in some dark shadow, his heart bounding at every slight desert rustle.

Then I stopped grinning.

'So, now you have lost the clue to the treasure, you come to me to see what I can do,' I said grimly.

'I have no alternative but to trust you,' she said.

'You sound bitter.'

'I don't like gunmen...'

'And I don't like...Oh, let's forget it for a while. Let's have a truce while we decide what we can do. I'm sure it's too late now to think of trailing the Noon Gang. That letter must have made some sort of sense to them. Can you remember what was in it?'

'I'll try, but first do you think you could trust me enough – now that we are temporary allies – to put that gun away. It's making me nervous.'

'Sorry, I had forgotten it was in my hand.' I slid the Peacemaker back under the poncho.

'The letter was impossible to read in parts.' She said, 'He must have been in a bad way when he wrote it. But from what I could read, the first bit was personal, how I was all he had left in the world and how he wanted to do something for me after he was gone by letting me have the gold, how he wanted to make amends... It's unimportant.

'The second part was how he'd gone prospecting with your father and the Mexicans, and how they'd struck it rich.

'All he mentioned about the location of the gold was "somewhere along the Gila", which doesn't tell us anything because the Gila is a mighty long river. He said they worked for nearly a year. They were afraid that if they returned before they had worked out the pocket they'd start a rush.

'Then his handwriting got very bad and I could not read it properly. At times it went right off the page. I remembered at one point he wrote: "Afterwards I took the mules and set out in the direction of the rising sun." He must have been referring to...'

'The murder of my father,' I said. The "rising sun" is significant because he probably killed them while they slept.' I could not control the bitterness in my voice.

She was silent a while. Then she said, 'After that there were some compass directions and Indian names. It was very confused, and I have not been able to trace them. I thought that as I travelled round I would have found something or some place that tied up with those names.'

'They must have meant something to Joshua Noon, seeing he took off so quickly,' I said. 'Can you remember any of them at all?'

'Some were in Apache, a few in English – like "Thunderbird Rock" – but they meant nothing. Some were in Spanish. I remember one because it was repeated several times...El Dedo de Dios. It means, The Finger of God. He ended up by saying "The gold is at the tip of the finger".'

'El Dedo de Dios,' I repeated, but it aroused no echo in my mind. It was a fanciful Spanish name such as many that were bestowed by the early explorers in the Sonora and Colorado regions and later forgotten.

31

'You've looked at maps, I suppose?'

'Yes. The best military ones. They are mostly blank, especially in the Gila Desert area. All I can gather is that it must have been pretty far west because I know he finally came out at Yuma.'

'Well, I can't think of anything now,' I said gloomily. 'Let's go and see Milton. Maybe he has a few ideas. He should know a lot about the territory.'

I had plenty to think about as I saddled up my horse in the moonlight. Just how far could I trust this girl with the beautiful face and a murderer for a father? It seemed all too straightforward all of a sudden. I was determined to be on my guard every second. I rolled up my blankets, slid the Winchester into its sheath by the saddle and mounted. I pulled Golden Dollar up behind me. She sat side saddle, with her arms around me. If it had been any other girl I would have found it pleasant.

CHAPTER 5

Light was streaking the sky when we finally reached Tombstone and were taken by Milton Homer to his office. Here we sat amongst printing machinery while he brewed up coffee. I spread a large map over the 'stone', at which the compositors work, and searched it for any signs that would lead to El Dedo de Dios.

'Careful you don't knock over that type,' admonished the reporter. 'My life wouldn't be worth a dime if it had to be set again.'

'I'll be careful,' I promised as my eyes followed the faintly marked trails that wandered into the great Gila Desert and were lost. Again I went over the clues that Golden Dollar remembered, but they meant no more to Milton than they did to me.

'I think there is only one person who can assist you,' he said finally. 'A Mexican called Pablo Martinez. He's a wanderer – an explorer and prospector. I understand he knows the Gila better than any man living.'

'Where do I find him?'

'If he is not in the wilderness, you may find him in Nogales. He might know something about El Dedo de Dios.'

'It's a slim chance, I muttered, 'but it's our only one. Can you ride, Golden Dollar?'

'Of course. I went to riding academy back East. I'll get what I need, then we'll buy another horse at the OK Corral and set off for Nogales.'

'Before you go, don't forget you promised me an exclusive story,' said Milton as we left the Tombstone

Epitaph.

'I'll not forget,' I replied. 'If I come out from the Gila in some other town, I'll telegraph it to you.'

As the sun rose we rode out of Tombstone, following a trail to the south. I had bought three more horses because, if we had a spare each, we could travel longer and faster. The two spares I had loaded with as many full waterbags as I could lay my hands on as well as a sack of flour and a small case of canned beans.

I noticed Golden Dollar was shivering under her cloak, yet in a few hours she would probably be dizzy with the heat. I only hoped she would be able to stand up to what lay ahead.

The main thing – in fact the only thing – that mattered was to find my father's gold. I suddenly wondered what would happen if, by some miracle, we got to it before the Noon Gang. No doubt Golden Dollar would want a share, yet it would be sacrilege to divide it with the daughter of the man who had killed his friends for it. To hell with Golden Dollar! I'd worry about that when we got the treasure. After all, she had only enlisted my help because she had no other way to turn.

I spurred my mount, increasing our pace. The track wound over undulating desert, often twisting through motionless groves of saguaros. Once a javelina darted out of a patch of Joshua tree in front of our horses. Golden Dollar's horse whinnied and plunged, but she controlled it with ease and I guessed it must have been a good academy where she learnt riding back East.

By noon our clothes were soaked with sweat and our faces burned from the reflected rays of the sun which smote us from sand and rock. Against this our sombreros were no protection. Often in the distance, over the wilderness of greasewood and mesquite and sand, water appeared to glitter temptingly. But it was the usual haunting mirage. Looking back, I noticed Golden Dollar

34

screwing up her eyes until they were almost closed.

'Here,' I said, reining up. 'Try this.'

I took out a small jar in which I had a mixture of candle black and tallow. I smeared this on her eyelids and just under her eyes.

'It does help,' she admitted. 'Where did you learn that?'

'It's an old cowboy trick,' I explained. 'I used to be a cowboy.'

'Was that before you began living by a gun?' she asked.

I was about to snarl a reply when we heard a dog howl, a long mournful wail of animal terror. I turned off the trail in the direction of the sound. Golden Dollar followed me. We cantered up an incline. At the top we found ourselves looking down on a shallow, saucer-shaped depression. Golden Dollar gave a cry – a sob of horror and fright.

About a hundred feet away there was the smouldering wreck of a wagon. By it were two shapes – human shapes – spread-eagled with their wrists and ankles tied to Apache lances that had been driven into the ground. The dog slunk round them and the charred wagon, yelping piteously.

'Stay here,' I said, drawing the Peacemaker. I slipped down from the saddle.

'You're not going to...'

'If necessary,' I snapped. 'It's what I'd want done to me.'

Trying to control the sick feeling in my guts, I approached the two grotesque bodies. There was an evil buzzing of flies. I noticed that the ground had been well trampled and little points of light reflected from spent cartridge cases.

It was a man and a woman. They had probably been young, maybe a couple out from the East seeking

35

their fortune in the new land. Luckily they were quite dead, so I holstered my gun.

According to the way the bloodstains had dried like cement in the sand, they must have been dead since early in the morning. I tried not to look at them as I cut the thongs that held them to the spear hafts...particularly I tried not to look at the woman.

Indian torture can turn the hardest stomach. It had transformed this couple into two scalped and mutilated monstrosities that I now had to cover.

I looked in the wreck of the wagon for a shovel and found one with a charred handle. It was still glowing in one place. I had to rub sand on it before I could use it. Then I began to scatter sand over the victims.

From the distance Golden Dollar watched. Her face was very white and she looked grotesque with the black eye make-up I had given her.

'Aren't you going to give them proper graves?' she cried out in a choking voice.

'There isn't time,' I replied. 'The war party must still be around these parts. We must move on as soon as possible.'

'You should do it properly,' she replied.

'Damn you,' I cried in anger. The horrible job I had to do, the danger I knew us to be in, and my dislike of the girl were almost too much for me. There in the heat, with the sinister fly buzz background, I felt like calling her every vile name I could think of. But I bit back the abuse and continued shovelling.

Suddenly she called again: 'Tashlin, I think there's something moving out there.'

From her vantage point on the low ridge she was pointing over my head, past what was left of the wagon, and in the direction of a sea of scrub. I threw down the shovel and ran clumsily over the soft sand and up the ridge.

'It was over there. I'm sure I saw something.'

I strained my eyes, but the scrub was motionless. Yet something told me danger was round us. It was as though death was breathing on my neck.

'Let's get out of here,' I said, climbing into the saddle.

'Aren't you going to finish...?' There was reproach in her voice.

'No!' I snapped. 'They're dead. Nothin' can hurt them now. But we're still alive, and I aim to keep it that way.'

As I spoke something flashed in the sun, something whistled close. It could have been a very fast bird, or –

'What was that?' Golden Dollar gasped.

I pointed behind us. In the yard-wide stem of a saguaro a feathered arrow was vibrating. Yet we had not seen a sign of the hidden bowman.

'See what I mean,' I cried, unsheathing the Winchester. 'Let's make a dash for it, back to the trail.'

But before I could turn my horse, our enemies materialised out of the scrub. Soundlessly they rose with their high-cheek-boned faces daubed with ghastly war paint. The nearest was about three hundred feet away. He had a rifle, no doubt looted from the wagon earlier on. I threw up the Winchester. There was not the time to aim that I should have liked, but I had to get the man with the rifle. I fired...and he disappeared with a thrashing motion into the scrub. It was like a man going under the surface of some strange sea.

'They are all round us,' cried Golden Dollar who had wheeled her horse. She was right. About twenty braves were spread out in a rough circle round our ridge. Without a word they were closing in, their bows drawn back, ready for use as soon as they were within range. I guessed they would aim for our horses. The mood they were in would make them try to take us alive.

'Come on,' I yelled, turning my horse. Our only hope was to break through the circle and get back on to the Nogales trail before they could get to wherever they had their horses hidden and follow us.

A volley of arrows hummed as we surged forward. I sent a shot crashing at a brave who stood directly in our path with his lance. He rolled out of the way, and we were back on the trail our lead animals snorting with fear.

From behind us came a wail of blood-chilling war cries. But if we had broken out, it was only to find ourselves in more trouble. The trail ahead was barred by a group of braves mounted on ponies. This was a bigger war party than I had guessed.

Not bothering to speak, I grabbed Golden Dollar's reins, kicked my mount viciously and we plunged off the trail on the opposite side. The mounted party began to follow us immediately over the plain. Their yells reached us through the quivering air and made us use our spurs unmercifully.

The scrub lashed us and our horses as we plunged through it. I was heading towards a small hillock that rose above the level of the plain about a mile to the south. I don't really know why I chose that direction. I guess one has to have some landmark to flee to.

Looking back over my shoulder I saw the Indians had fanned out. On their desert bred ponies they were gradually overtaking us. No doubt the rest of the party would follow as soon as they got their mounts.

We neared the hillock. I could see it was scattered with boulders. At least we could make a stand here.

As we reached its steep approach, the horses began to stumble. I halted, swung out of the saddle and lifted Golden Dollar down. Then, holding her wrist, I led the way up the steep slope.

Often sand and pebbles slid away beneath us and we'd sprawl forward, cutting ourselves on sharp rock crops. By the time we reached the top, we were bleeding from dozens of cuts and scratches. Looking back I saw our pursuers were only a couple of hundred yards from the point where we had abandoned our mounts.

I made Golden Dollar lie flat in the shade of a rock. I rested the Winchester on another and took careful aim at the leading brave. It was hard aiming. The glare of the desert strained my eyes and the dancing air made it difficult to keep him in my sights. And I had to be quick! There were at least ten of his companions to deal with after I'd killed him.

The Winchester cracked. I must have hit his horse in the foreleg because the Indian came tumbling over its head and it went down. He tried to regain his feet, but my second shot got him.

The other braves paused, then dismounted. They took up position behind lumps of rock in the shadow of grease wood. All were armed with rifles and soon bullets were ricocheting about us. They left long silver marks on the worn rocks behind which we sheltered.

I did not want to waste ammunition, but I had to keep them at bay. I guessed their tactics would be to keep us pinned down until their companions arrived. Then they would worm from cover to cover until it would be possible to take us in a final fanatical rush.

I handed the Peacemaker to Golden Dollar.

'Keep watch behind us,' I said. 'They'll be trying to crawl round the hill. I don't want to be rushed from the rear.'

'I thought the Indians were your father's friends,' she muttered angrily.

'Red Cloud was his blood brother,' I said. 'But these are Geronimo's men from the East. I can tell by their paint.'

In my sights I could see a face with a white bar painted across its cruel broad features. I squeezed the trigger with even pressure, and another brave went to the Happy Hunting Ground.

'How are we going to get out of this?' asked Golden Dollar in a voice that was almost normal. She seemed to have mastered her fear, and was now crouched behind a rock like myself, scanning the landscape over the barrel of the Colt .45.

'I dunno,' I replied honestly. 'I guess we must just concentrate on stayin' alive minute by minute. Who knows the militia may turn up.'

The militia didn't turn up for those two we found,' she replied sombrely.

A rifle spoke. A bullet smacked a rock near us, then whined into the brassy sky.

I continued probing the desert with my eyes, ready to shoot at the slightest movement. In my mind I could imagine the braves squirming through the brush like snakes.

Until their reinforcements came I did not expect a head-on charge up the steep slope. The Apache is probably one of the bravest as well as the meanest fighting men in the world. But despite his code of high personal courage, he is not a fool. He has no more wish to be killed than the next man, and only indulges in suicidal charges if there is no other way.

If time was on their side they could keep us on top of the hill until the sun did their work for them. Our water was still on our horses which had wandered off into the greasewood. It would not be long before we felt the torment of desert thirst. By the position of the sun I knew it must be noon. The hellish, blistering afternoon lay ahead of us. I wondered grimly if we would be alive when the cool evening came.

'Funny, I never expected it might come like this,' mused Golden Dollar. Then she was silent again. I pumped a couple of shots in the direction of what I thought was the gleam of a rifle barrel. Chips of rock flew up near it and it hastily disappeared.

'I've heard tales about the Indians, but I never realised how cruel they could be,' she said a little later.

'We are not blameless either,' I answered. 'There is cruelty on every side. It was the whitemen who started the habit of scalping, to prove how many Indians they'd exterminated – like pest hunters. The habit caught on with the Indians who wished to revenge themselves. Both sides are bad. We've taken their land, they've murdered settlers.'

'I don't care about sides,' said Golden Dollar. 'I just want to stay alive...and find that gold.'

I was almost surprised that I had forgotten about the gold, the very reason for our journey and this predicament. Time passed slow second by slow second. Several times I fired at some movement, but the Apaches seemed very patient. They were content to wait. Meanwhile the heat was making our heads spin.

'I feel as though I'm on fire,' murmured Golden Dollar weakly.

Her words gave me an idea. Careful not to expose myself to the Indian snipers, I pushed together a little mound of tinder-dry thorn. Then I set it alight.

'Aren't you hot enough already?' she asked derisively.

I was too busy to reply to her foolish remarks. A column of smoke began to ascend, and I threw sand on the thorn to make sure it would not burn too fast. It continued to smoke just as I wanted it.

'This Apache trick might beat them at their own game,' I said. 'There is a chance that the militia may be hunting for this war party...well, it's the only thing I can think of doing.'

My smoke signal certainly had an effect on the Apaches. Maybe they figured I really had someone to signal to, but whatever they thought they seemed very determined to finish us off. A fusillade of bullets whistled round us, forcing us to keep our heads down.

Glancing over a rock, I saw that three of them, under the covering fire of their comrades, were following our tracks up the steep incline. It was going to be now or never. I took the risk and stood up with the Winchester, firing as fast as I could. I heard the crash of the Peacemaker, and there was Golden Dollar blazing away beside me.

Two Indians dropped in their tracks from our bullets. The leader paused – he was close to us now – and his pause was fatal. My rifle cracked and he went spinning down the slope like a human top. The firing from the Apaches stopped. There was an eerie silence, broken occasionally by the whimpering of one of the men I had shot.

'They'll wait for the others,' I said. 'We did pretty well then. We've cut down their numbers by half. Throw some more thorn on the fire.'

Golden Dollar did so. Then we just waited on the hillock while the wounded Apache continued to moan.

CHAPTER 6

More time passed. At regular intervals I peered over my rock, scanning the desert before our vantage point. There was no sign of the Indians, though once or twice I thought I heard them whistling to each other. Behind me Golden Dollar was keeping watch with the Peacemaker. The heat made my head swim. I felt giddy and weak, and waves of sickness swept me from time to time.

Lying on top of this hillock we had no shelter from the sun. Beneath our bodies the rocks gave off heat as though they were ovens. I felt all I wanted to do was close my eyes and dream of drifting along in a stream of ice cold water.

The sound of a pebble hitting another roused me. I turned. To my horror I saw that Golden Dollar was sprawled unconscious, and beyond her limp form there was poised an Apache brave. He seemed to blot out half the sky. With an exultant whoop he leapt at me before I could swing the Winchester round at him. A knife gleamed like a long fragment of mirror in his hand. Next second we were grappling together.

His body was slippery with sweat and greasy war paint. Within seconds he had forced me down on my back. Hissing with evil triumph, he gripped my hair with his left hand while he raised his knife high in his right.

I summoned all the strength I could muster and writhed to one side. The knife missed my throat by inches. Just within my line of vision I saw the pistol that must have been laid down by Golden Dollar before she passed out. Frantically I grabbed for it, but the Apache was too quick for me. He kicked it away with his moccasined foot.

As a last desperate attempt to hold on to life I struggled to raise my hands to his throat. He just laughed and raised the knife again. I changed my tactics and managed to seize his wrist. Now it was a trial of strength with the knife inching towards me.

Suddenly there was a high pitched report. The Apache's face melted from a mask of hatred to an almost comical one of bewilderment. Then he rolled off me and lay still.

I sat up, and saw Golden Dollar on her knees with a tiny pistol in her hand. It was the Derringer she kept in her garter and with which she had threatened me at the Birdcage those few nights ago.

'I'm sorry...I must have fainted...' she muttered, looking with horror at the corpse of the brave she had just dispatched.

There as no time to comfort her. I struggled to my feet to see if other Indians were coming, but the scene was strangely still. The dead warrior must have come alone on this assassination attempt. No doubt he wanted to win extra honour for himself.

Somewhere a rifle cracked. A bullet whined overhead. If our enemies were out of sight, at least they were still as dangerous as ever.

'Thanks for your help,' I said to Golden Dollar as we crouched down again. That was pretty brave.'

'I was just damn terrified,' she replied with a shudder. 'I did what I did without thinking.'

Guessing at what she must be feeling, I pushed the body of the Indian over the edge of the rock on which it had been sprawled. It rolled limply away down the slope, the limbs flopping like those of a broken doll.

I had just settled down over the Winchester when I heard the faint echo of distant gunfire. I looked over the plain in the direction of the Nogales trail. At first all I could see was desert, then through the heat haze I made out a scattered band of horsemen coming fast in our direction. It was the other half of the war party which I had figured had remained by the trail to ambush the Nogales stage.

My first thought was that they were coming to finish us off. We may have given a good account of ourselves, but these reinforcements would overwhelm us. But seconds later I discerned behind the galloping braves a bobbing line of blue.

The sound of shooting was nearer. Soon I was able to see the details of the fleeing Apaches, even to the decorations streaming from their lances.

Now the detachment of cavalry became clearer. They were riding like demons through the scrub and sage in open formation, firing their carbines as they swept along.

Closer at hand, the Indians who had us bushed ran back to their horses and joined the main body of braves as it swept past our hillock in confusion. I speeded them on their way by sending as many slugs after them as I could. To me it was the greatest sight I had seen in my life. The clear call of the bugler was the sweetest sound I had ever heard. I tried to cheer, but all I could manage was a stupid croak from between my swollen lips.

* * *

It was the best meal the Nogales hotel could provide. Golden Dollar and I were sharing it with Captain Marvin Dexter, the leader of the cavalry troop that had saved us from the Apaches the day before.

'Your health, ma'am,' the gallant captain was saying. He raised his wine glass in one hand and twirled his moustache with the other. Golden Dollar glowed with pleasure. No wonder the captain's eyes twinkled. Rested from her ordeal, and in a new and very revealing gown, Golden Dollar was now a very different girl to the one the

45

troopers had found with me on the hillock.

The cavalry had been on a patrol which was on the lookout for one of Germonimo's raiding parties which had swept into the territory just north of the border. It was my smoke signal that had alerted them. They had taken it for an Indian signal, but this did not matter. It had saved the day for us.

Now the troopers were whooping it up in the border town of Nogales, swaggering in the Mexican taverns and sporting houses. I could see that Captain Marvin Dexter would also like to whoop it up – with Golden Dollar. He was in dress uniform complete with sword, and his moustaches were waxed until they stuck out like the horns of a steer. For her part, she was losing no opportunity to flirt with the handsome hero. Well, she could flirt with him as much as she liked for all I cared. I was only interested in finding another link in the chain that would lead me to my father's gold.

In fact, I would have been delighted if the captain had taken this girl off my hands leaving me to get on with the search. Once she had explained about her father's letter to Pablo Martinez she would be no further use on the treasure hunt.

As I sat there, sipping my wine while my two companions made eyes at each other, I wondered how Joshua Noon and his gang were getting on. As they had taken mules they would not be travelling very fast. Another point in my favour might be that even with the letter they would have difficulty in finding El Dedo de Dios, wherever it might be.

My immediate task was to find Pablo Martinez.

'Excuse me,' I said when the main course was over. 'I must go out on business.'

The captain looked delighted at this piece of information. 'Don't mention it, my dear sir. I am sure this charming lady will be safe in my company.'

'I only hope you'll be safe in hers,' I said, and left the hotel. I turned into the nearest bar. In the light of oil lamps I could see a few Mexicans sitting about drinking tequila.

I ordered a beer and asked the bar-keep: 'Do you know Senor Pablo Martinez?'

'Ah yes, *señor*. Who along the border does not know Pablo Martinez! A big man, *señor* – big heart, big stomach...that's Pablo. He is very brave, like the puma. He is very loving, thirteen children...'

They tell me he travels in the desert.'

'Si. He goes off, usually when there is an infante coming. Then one day he is back. Sometimes with a bit of silver, sometimes with gold. Who can say where he finds it.'

'Is he in town – where can I find him?'

The barkeep gave me directions and I strolled through the cool evening until I found myself at an abode house on the outskirts of town.

On the doorstep sat an immense man with a glass in his hand. His face was upturned to the stars with a gentle smile on it. From inside came the sound of a woman crooning a Spanish lullaby.

'Are you *Señor* Martinez?'

'Si, *señor*. How can I be of assistance...but first come and sit down and we will have a drink under these most glittering stars. Maria, tequila for our guest.'

I sat beside him. A pleasant looking Mexican woman brought the tequila bottle, glasses, salt and the hot red sauce which were all necessary in the tequila ritual. The sauce was to enliven your taste and encourage a thirst. The salt you sprinkled on the back of your hand. You then licked this off and immediately downed the torrid cactus liquor. It made my eyes water, but a comforting glow began to spread through my body.

I saw that at least part of the barman's description

of Pablo Martinez was right. He was big. His belly sagged good naturedly over his belt. His face was as round as a cannonball and his arms were those of a giant. He took a slug of tequila, sighed, patted his stomach, lit a cigar and was ready to talk business.

Without mentioning the gold, I explained how we wanted to trace something in the Gila Desert, that we had a few clues but we needed expert help.

'It must be gold you seek, otherwise who else but a madman would want to go into the Gila,' he said. 'Will you pay well if I help?'

'Of course.'

'I should want my payment left in the bank here in Nogales, with an agreement that if I do not return within a month my wife can draw it out.'

'I'd agree to that. But you certainly don't take chances, *señor*.'

'Not with a man who has a reputation as a gunfighter, Senor Tashlin. Not that I mean disrespect.'

'I understand,' I said shortly. Even here the name Tashlin was associated with gunplay and violence.

We drank more tequila. We agreed on terms, and then I told him about Golden Dollar's letter. It was only when I mentioned the name El Dedo de Dios that his interest quickened.

'The Finger of God,' he mused. 'That is strange. I do know of a landmark of that name. It was given to a pinnacle of rock by an old Spanish explorer. He was probably the first white man to cross the Gila. Most of the names he gave to places are forgotten now. You would not find them on the maps. But I learned some of them from my father, who was also a wanderer. Are there any other names, *señor*?'

'Some Indian names. I can't remember them off hand.'

'It is of no matter,' he said looking at me full in the

face. 'I am sure I know El Dedo de Dios. Some time ago some prospectors died near there. It was said they were killed by the Apaches and that they were carrying much gold.'

'Oh, yes?' I said, trying to look steadily back into his coal black eyes.

'Oh yes, *Señor* Tashlin,' he laughed. 'You wish to find your father's gold, yes?'

'Yes, you're dead right,' I answered. It was no good trying to fool a man like Pablo.

'Good. Now we know each other. I am your man if you deposit five hundred dollars in the bank as we agreed...Americano dollars, of course.

'Okay. But it's a lot of Americano dollars, *señor*.'

'But if I lose my life, then it is a very few dollars for my life. And you can trust me. Ask anyone. I am a true man. I shall not betray you as maybe your father' s comrade betrayed him.'

Looking at the smiling, bulky man I knew I could rely on him. There was an air of sincerity about him. So I explained the whole story to him, leaving nothing out. When I told him about the part Joshua Noon was playing in the melodrama, he said: 'We have the advantage over them. I know the Gila better than any living man. We shall get to El Dedo first. Let us start at sun up, as soon as we can get provisions.'

'That's fine by me.'

'Do you want this dancehall girl to come with us?'

'No. Just you and I are for this trip, Pablo.'

'You are right, *señor*. The Gila is no place for a woman.'

We shook hands and I went back to the hotel. As I entered the lobby I met Captain Marvin Dexter leaving somewhat unsteadily. He scowled when he saw me.

'You had a pleasant evening, I trust,' I said, suddenly annoyed that I felt a strange stab of something that might almost be jealousy.

'It was fine and dandy until a few minutes ago,' he muttered drunkenly. 'That gal is a she-devil...' And he rolled out into the Mexican night. As I went past I caught sight of a livid hand mark on his cheek. Obviously Golden Dollar had not found his attentions all that acceptable.

I felt my heart lift. Then with sudden cold sense I shrugged. After all, what did it matter. I would not be seeing Golden Dollar again. I sat down at a bureau and wrote her a short note and gave it to the clerk to deliver in the morning. By the time she read it I would be heading towards the Gila with Pablo Martinez. There was no place in my life for the daughter of the man who had murdered my father.

CHAPTER 7

It was mid-morning. The heat was cruel. A trickle of sweat ran down my back and my eyes were sore with being screwed up against the glare. On the trail ahead rode Pablo Martinez, leading a couple of packhorses piled high with provisions and Mexican water skins. I lead another. We were heading north-west, and in the shimmering distance there rose a mountain peak.

'That mountain is called Babqui-vari,' Pablo called back from under his enormous sombrero. 'We go round its southern slopes, then head north. If we keep up this pace we will outdistance your friend Joshua Noon. He cannot know the desert as well as Pablo Martinez, nor can he move so fast with his mules. Anyway, he will not know you are following...'

'I hope you're right,' I said. 'But Joshua is a mighty cunning hombre. I'd rather have dealings with a side-winder than that cold-eyed son of a coyote. He makes my blood run cold when I think of him.'

'That is something, coming from a man like you,' said Pablo. 'I thought you professional gunmen did not know fear like us ordinary men.'

I bit back an oath. I was sick to the heart of the label 'professional gunman'. Until I had started this hunt for the lost gold I had tried to forget my reputation. I was working on a small ranch in New Mex and I had tried to forget my career with a Colt.

So I rode on, brooding on my past and disliking it more and more. Then I began to brood on why I was brooding. Was I getting soft? Now I was getting close to the thirties, was some sort of change taking place inside me. Before, when I had gained my reputation with a gun, I had not worried about it. If I was honest with myself there were times when I was proud of my coolness and skill. I had been pushed into the role of gunfighter, but I had accepted it without question. Now I was full of doubts, especially after that kid in the Las Cruces saloon...

My thoughts were interrupted by a sound behind me. It was the muffled drumming of hooves. I swung round in the saddle and squinted down the trail. I could just make out a distant dot of a horseman. Pablo pulled out a brass tube from his saddlebag. It was an old Navy telescope. He extended it to full length and focussed it carefully. Then he laughed so that his big white teeth flashed in his fat swarthy face.

'It is your lady friend, *señor*,' he chuckled. 'Maybe she objects to being left behind, yes?'

As she approached I saw that she was wearing the clothes of a cowboy, pants and all. She was certainly very different from the perfectly gowned beauty I had seen singing on the stage of the Birdcage Theatre.

She reined up viciously so that spurts of sand flew from under her mount's hooves.

'You lowdown, chiselin' outlaw!' she snarled as she pushed her sombrero to the back of her head. Her eyes sparkled with hate as she looked at me.

'So, you thought you could leave me out, you rat,' she continued. 'Well, let me tell you, you cheatin' skunk...' And she went on with a fluency that even Milton Homer would have envied. When she finally stopped it was only because her breath had given out.

'Did you get my note?' I asked. 'I left it for you with the hotel clerk...'

'Sure, and I tore it up in his face,' she snapped. 'You won't get away just by leaving farewell notes, you twister. To think I told you about my father's treasure...'

52

'Your father's treasure...' I sneered.

'It's mine as much as it is yours,' she replied savagely. 'So let me inform you, you connivin' son of a rattlesnake, that I'm comin' along whether you like it or not. The only way you can stop me is with a bullet...and maybe even a gun-slinger like you might stop at shootin' women!'

And so it went on. We shouted at each other in the heat, the sweat streaming down our faces and our bodies tense with rage.

It was Pablo who restored order.

'Come, *señor*, *señorita*,' he purred. To act like children is unwise. We cannot go back now, we waste too much time. Let us continue together as good comrades. Why fight over gold that is still hidden away.'

His words calmed us down. Realising that Golden Dollar was with us now, whether I liked it or not, I rode at a sulky distance behind. She rode up front with Pablo, being as charming as possible with him and making him laugh frequently – no doubt to annoy me.

But even though he was being sociable, the Mexican kept up the pace. The horses trotted steadily and the peak loomed closer and closer. Pablo was certainly an excellent guide. The trail seemed to have run out now, but he kept on without hesitation. At noon we halted to rest the horses and drink some tepid water.

'By sundown we should reach New Jerusalem,' he announced.

'What's New Jerusalem?' I asked.

'It's a strange little settlement on the edge of the Gila Desert,' he explained. 'A religious group settled there sometime back. I think they are loco, but it is the last outpost we shall see before we reach El Dedo de Dios.'

As he spoke we little realised that New Jerusalem was nearly the last outpost we should see ever!

* * *

The sky was as red as fire as the sun balanced on the western rim of the desert. Through the deepening gloom we followed the trail towards a collection of shacks silhouetted against the sunset. As we approached we passed several crude signs. The first said 'New Jerusalem' in blistered paint, the second announced 'The Wages of Sin is Death', and the third one advised us to prepare to meet our doom.

Several flea-bitten dogs ran towards us, snarling viciously and making the weary horses twitch in alarm. We drew up in a square surrounded by the crazy, sun-warped buildings. Nothing stirred, but I had a curious tingle down my spine. I was sure that somewhere there was a gun pointing in my direction.

'It's like a ghost town,' said Golden Dollar in a hushed voice.

I casually turned my head. In the deep shadow of a shack I saw a wild looking youth with hair down to his eyes peering at us over the twin barrels of a shotgun. I had a notion he would enjoy pulling the trigger. I wondered how many other citizens of New Jerusalem were hidden with their sights trained on us.

Something told me the outcasts who had settled here on the edge of the Gila were itching to send a volley at us. Then I could imagine them taking the gear from our horses, stripping our clothes from our bodies, eagerly going through our pockets. I had seen mad little communities like this before and I avoided them when I could.

Suddenly a tall figure stalked out from one of the shacks. He wore sandals and a filthy robe that reached his knees. His unkempt hair hung down to his shoulders, and his beard almost covered his belly.

'I am Brother Jeremiah,' he announced. 'What do you strangers seek with the Lambs of the Lord?'

'Water and shelter, *señor*,' answered Pablo.

54

'We have few strangers here,' said Brother Jeremiah. 'We have renounced the world of sin and vice. We have turned our faces from our enemies. We have built New Jerusalem on the very edge of the wilderness. Strangers are not welcome. They scoff at our righteous ways, they carry sin with them like an infection...' He went on and on. Out of the corner of my eye I saw more Lambs of the Lord sidling forward with their guns pointing straight at us.

'If we could stay the night here, *señor*, we would be happy to pay for our accommodation,' said Pablo when Brother Jeremiah finally paused.

'A donation to the Funds of the Temple would certainly prove that you are not too ungodly,' he said, his eyes suddenly looking crafty. You understand that here we must be careful who we welcome. The desert is the home of outlaws and blasphemers. We have suffered for our faith. We have been driven from town to town for the sake of our belief until there is only the desert left. Yet the Lord will look down on his Lambs, and our day will come when we, the righteous, are the only ones saved from the flaming pit.'

To cut him short, Pablo tossed the leader of the Lambs three silver dollars.

'Blessings on thee,' he muttered. 'You two can sleep in that empty hut, the lady can sleep in my family house...'

One of the Lambs snickered from the shadows. Like other similar sects, the Lambs no doubt had some curious customs in regard to the sharing of women.

'She will be safe with my handmaidens,' continued Brother Jeremiah warming to the theme. 'She shall be anointed with oil and brought before the throne of righteousness...'

'Thank you, but I would prefer to remain with my...with my husband,' said Golden Dollar in desperation.

She turned to me with a look of appeal on her face.

Brother Jeremiah looked sad. No doubt he had looked forward to showing this golden haired girl the righteous customs of New Jerusalem. But you can't win every time, even if you are a Lamb of the Lord.

Pablo and I attended to the horses, tethering them to a rail by the crazy hut in which we were to spend the night. Watched by the community, which had now sneaked up out of the shadows, Golden Dollar prepared the evening meal of tamales and beans.

When we sat down to eat it I teased her by saying: 'Pass the bread, wife,' or, 'Make coffee, Mrs Tashlin.'

She looked daggers at me, but as a temporary husband in name only I was still preferable to the ragged fanatics who watched our every move in eerie silence.

There were a score of grown men, some skinny, mean-looking youths and a dozen dirty kids. The womenfolk looked burnt out and old before their time, yet their eyes had the same crazy fire as Brother Jeremiah's.

'Wouldn't it have been better for us to camp out?' I asked Pablo softly as we ate our evening meal.

'Not with the Apaches on the warpath,' he replied. 'Here, *señor*, they may be mad but at least there is safety in numbers. And also I fear that this so-dirty place is built round the last well before El Dedo de Dios.'

After we finished our beans the adult Lambs melted away, leaving the kids to fight over the scraps. In the mean hut we rolled ourselves up in our blankets, and I took the precaution of laying the Peacemaker within easy reach.

Golden Dollar lay as far away from me as she could manage, and when I joked 'Good night, Mrs Tashlin!' she responded with an unladylike 'Go to hell!'

A minute later she said in a different sort of voice: 'Bill, what's that scrabbling noise?'

'I guess it sounds too loud to be a bug,' I said.

'Probably a rat.'

There was a little scream from the other end of the hut, then Golden Dollar wailed: 'O Lord, what have I done to have to spend the night surrounded by rats in the same hut with a mean-minded gunslinger!'

'Senorita, do not worry about the rats. They would only bite you if you were dead...they are part of Creation and as such .have their place,' said Pablo.

'You are very philosophical, Senor Martinez,' replied Golden Dollar. 'You have explained the rats, but how do you explain the gunman?'

'Hah, for such men there is no explanation that I know of,' he said. 'Senor Tashlin, can you explain your-self?'

'Nope,' I said. 'I guess no man can explain himself. And as far as gunslinger s are concerned, there must be a different explanation for each one. Some start livin' by the Colt for pride, some for greed, some for lust, some maybe even for honour...'

'How could anyone take up such a life for honour?' scoffed Golden Dollar.'

'I saw a gunman born once,' I said. 'It was certainly honour that made him start totin' the "Hardware from Hartford." I'll tell you about it.'

CHAPTER 8

'It happened when I was still quite a kid,' I said, rolling a smoke in the dark. 'My father was runnin' a store in a little one-hoss minin' town south of the Sonora Plateau. It had the misleadin' name of Hope City...there was no city and damn little hope. Law and order had not caught up with it, but if a bit was required my old man would pin a tin star on his shirt and deal it out on the spot with the help of his shotgun.

'The time I'm tellin' you about there was a gunman stayin' in Hope City. He was called Kid Summer, an' he was a tall hombre with fair hair worn like Bill Hickok. He looked the best natured guy in the world until he got into an argument an' then his eyes would sorta turn to ice and when he went for his Pater son his hand was so fast you just couldn't see it. At the time he was in Hope City that gun had accounted for a dozen guys, no countin' Indians.

'Well, the Kid used to hang out in the Nugget Saloon, drinking beer and takin' a hand at cards now an' then. There was always a group of admirers hangin' round him in the hope of seein' some fancy gun work.

'I think my father was quite glad to have him in town. When there's a top gun around the usual hell-raisers are inclined to take it easy so the town becomes more peaceful, unless some crazy guy decides to pick a quarrel with the slinger so he can snatch his reputation.

'That's just what happened in the Nugget Saloon. There was a miner called Bernstein who rather fancied his chances with his Navy Colt. One day he got liquored up at the Last Chance Bar with his mates from the diggings.

Pretty soon they got to talkin' about gun fightin' and unfortunately for Bernstein he had a theory. He figured that the reason gun fighters won was because they had big reputations. This made other people nervy and unable to shoot straight.

'Fortified with Red Eye, he crossed over to the Nugget to test out his idea. The Kid was drinkin' a beer and lookin' at a fan of cards in his hand. Bernstein took one look at him, an' told him he was a cheatin' rattlesnake.

'The Kid clambered to his feet kinda slow. There was a sad smile on his face, an' everyone tried to move back out of range without actually runnin' away.

' "You weren't smilin' when you said that, mister," said the Kid, who was known for his witty remarks.

'It was over quickly. The Kid waited calmly until Bernstein went for his gun, then he went into action. The guns went off almost together, but the Kid was steady and accurate and his bullet caught the miner in the middle of the chest, toppling him right over. He was very dead when he hit the floor.

'I remember the Kid looked at him with a funny expression on his face as he holstered the Paterson. There was a long silence which was broken by a voice speaking broken English.

' "You are an uncivilised pig!" it said. "Because you can shoot down a drunken man, you think you pretty damn big, eh? You make me disgusted."

'The hombre who was tellin' the Kid his opinion of him was a young punk the miners called Frenchy, on account of the fact he was French. His real name was Jacques St. Cloud, and he was supposed to be from a family that had a title before the French Revolution. In order to retrieve the family fortunes the poor coyote had come out West prospectin'. He'd had no luck and his clothes were nearly rags. He'd sold everythin' of value, his father's watch, his mother's ring, and all that remained was the old St. Cloud duelling pistols which he kept in a battered leather case. He said he'd starve to death before he'd sell them, but he needn't have bothered – no one in Hope City would have been seen with the old muzzleloaders.

' "So I disgust you, monsieur," said the Kid very softly after a long silence. "Let me tell you one thing – if you were man enough to wear a gun you'd be a corpse now. You only shoot off your mouth because you know that I wouldn't shoot an unarmed man. So run off, Frenchy, before I forget my principles. Vamos!"

'Frenchy went red in the face, realisin' he'd made a fool of himself, so he shambled out into the street where he was sick because he'd never seen a man shot before.

'In the Nugget the Kid sat down again, picked up his cards an' – you may not believe it – found he had a Royal Flush.

'Later I remember my old man tryin' to talk some sense into the young Frenchman. "You don't savvy the way things are here," he said. "The Kid was entitled to shoot Bernstein in self defence..."

' "In France," said Frenchy, "They would have fought like gentlemen, with rapiers and seconds. Here they act like brutes. My grandfather died in a duel of honour, but it was to protect the name of a lady, not over a drunken bar brawl."

' "This ain't France," my Dad reminded him.

' "This is a new land an' you gotta take it or leave it. An' if you don't want to leave it via the local cemetery, keep clear of the Kid."

'Well, Frenchy went on an' on about how barbaric everythin' was, and how he could not understand how men enjoyed murderin' each other with Colts. An', I remember, in a funny sorta way, I liked him, and I knew my old man did, too. He could imagine him in Paris, I

60

guess, surrounded by his admirin' sisters, writin' poetry, an' dreamin' of findin' a fortune that would make his family rich again. I guess the life of a minin' camp had come as a nasty surprise.

' "Why do you stay in Hope City if you don't like it?" I asked him, but even though I was a shaver I knew the answer. As for Frenchy, he turned a sort of pink colour and went back to his digging without a word.

The answer was, of course, that the poor punk was in love. It's a bad enough state for any guy to be in, but with a sensitive character like him it was a disaster, seein' how the girl of his dreams was a dancer called the Texas Rose who every night gave the customers an eyeful over the footlights of the Hope City Palace Theatre.

'Each night, when the miners relaxed after a hard day's toil by gettin' blind drunk an' whistlin' at the Palace Theatre gals, Frenchy would sit in the front row just livin' for the moment when Texas Rose came on to the stage. Sometimes he went without food to save the money for this nightly view of his princess.

The Texas Rose was tall an' very shapely an' she had long black hair and a sorta smile that would make the miners take pot shots at the roof – and Frenchy almost burst into tears. To him she was somethin' out of this world, though to everyone else she was a good-time gal with a certain style and a likin' for big spenders. What made the drama more complete was that the Texas Rose was the reason for the Kid stayin' in town, though I guess he had a lot more success with the dancer than the lovelorn French boy.

'It was a week after Bernstein had been shot that the Kid was in the Nugget Saloon in a very good mood.

He was tellin' his hangers-on what a devil of a fellow he was with the ladies, and with the Texas Rose in particular. In fact, I think he added some quite amusin' details...

'At this point Frenchy jumps up and hollers: "No gentleman would talk about a lady like that in a bar." His words made the Kid double up with laughter. He nearly choked on his beer. But Frenchy was gonna have his say. Red-faced, speaking in terrible English, he told the Kid what he thought of him, his family and his remote ancestors, an' he finished by sayin': "I demand that you take back your words and that you apologise to the lady."

' "The Lady...!" roared the Kid, nearly purple in the face. "The Texas Rose a lady! That's the best I've heard for a long time..."

'This final remark was too much for the gallant Frenchman. He threw his whisky neatly into the Kid's face – glass an' all.

Well, the Kid was on his feet and his gun was out quicker'n a rattler can strike. But he didn't fire. Instead he slowly sheathed his Paterson and said in a loud voice: "You know I don't shoot unarmed men, so I'm givin' you a chance. I'll be on Main Street at ten tomorrow mornin'. I'll be waitin' for you. If you have any guts you'll find yourself a gun."

'Later that night Frenchy came to my Dad's store, beggin' to borrow a Colt. He was all set to fight for the Texas Rose's honour, but he hadn't the cash to buy a gun.

' "Sorry, son," said my old man, "but you won't get a gun in this town. It'd be murder to let you have one. Pack your roll and hit the road and thank the Lord you're still alive." '

' "A St. Cloud doesn't run," he muttered.

' "Yeah, but you can't fight without a gun," said my Dad. "Anyways, I always thought you were dead against this barbaric gunplay."

'Frenchy laughed bitterly, and wandered off. I knew he wouldn't get a gun in Hope City because my father had passed round the word that he'd pin on his star and arrest anyone supplyin' Frenchy with a gun.

'Just the same I went to Main Street next mornin', just to see the Kid walkin' up an' down. Quite a few citizens had foregathered under the verandahs of the shanties that lined the one street of the town. Among those present was the Texas Rose, no doubt pretty elated over the fact there was a gallant boy who would throw a drink in the Kid's face for her sake.

'I saw that the Kid was standin' alone at the far end of the street. He was in his waistcoat, havin' left off his frock coat so he could reach his gun easier.

'As it got near ten there was a funny sorta silence. I remember a little dog paddin' down the street.

'Nobody thought Frenchy would turn up, but there was somethin' about the lonely figure of the Kid that gave us afeelin' of fear.

'Suddenly there was a soft gasp, and all eyes turned from the Kid to the opposite end of Main Street. There was the French boy walkin' steadily down the middle of the street. In the mornin' sunlight he seemed quite good lookin' with the breeze rufflin' the hair over his forehead.

' "What varmint gave him a Colt?" my father muttered, but it was too late to do anythin' about it. Then I saw what was in his holster. It was a powder and ball pistol like they used a hundred years ago, one of the St. Cloud duelling pistols.

'I knew that Frenchy wouldn't stand a chance with that single-shot old cannon, and I remember I wanted to run out and stop him, but there was somethin' in his face that held me back. He was deathly white, and yet there was a strange fever in his eyes.

'I guess the Texas Rose had the same idea. "Jacky, he'll murder you," she cried, but Jacques St. Cloud walked past her without givin' her a look. The sweat glistened on his forehead, but his step was steady.

'By now the Kid was amblin' forward from his

63

end. Sooner or later one of these two would go for his gun, and then it would be over within seconds. A pity about Frenchy, I thought. The Texas Rose's reputation was not much of a thing to give your life over.

'The Kid came on. His hand brushed his holster and his eyes were set on the French boy's face.

'Suddenly Jacques St. Cloud went for his ancient gun. Being such an odd shape, it seemed to stick in the modern holster and he had quite a job to get it out.

'Meanwhile the Kid drew and fired, an' his bullet fanned the French boy's cheek.

'He was just gonna fire again when he saw the clumsy gun that Frenchy was struggling with. His face split into a laugh.

'I don't know if he would have put the Paterson away, seein' what his enemy was armed with, but there was a roar like a charge of blastin' powder goin' off, and the laugh seemed to freeze on the Kid's face. His eyes rolled, the Paterson dropped, for a second he clawed the big hole in his breast, then he pitched forward.

'Jacques St. Cloud walked up to the body. No one said a word, but when the Texas Rose ran up to him and tried to put her arms round him he pushed her roughly to one side. There was a thoughtful look on his face, and even I could see that the Texas Rose interested him no more. Somethin' much deeper than love had happened to him.

'He dropped the smoking old family duelling pistol, bent over the Kid and unbuckled his gunbelt. He strapped it round his own hips, then he picked up the Kid's Paterson and placed it in the holster.

'Everyone was so surprised as Jacques St. Cloud walked round to the town corral, where he saddled the Kid's horse, that no one had anythin' to say.

'It was only when the Frenchman cantered out of town that the talk began to buzz. It ain't everyday you see a gunfighter born. When Jack Cloud, the famous gun-fighter, met his match in Laredo two years later there were nine notches on the butt of his gun.'

* * *

The story over, we pulled our blankets tighter round ourselves and settled down to sleep. Soon I knew by the regular breathing of Golden Dollar that she slept, then Pablo began to snore gently. Just before I went off I put out my hand and touched the Peacemaker to reassure myself. At least I had never cut notches on its butt.

CHAPTER 9

I cannot remember what it was that woke me. It might have been the creak of the leather-hinged door, or it might have been a stifled cry from Golden Dollar. Whatever it was, I opened my eyes a fraction, but made no other movement.

A few inches from my face I saw a pair of fancy riding boots with big Mexican silver spurs. It was not the kind of footwear worn by the Lambs.

Around me there was some sort of bustle. I could hear Golden Dollar protesting about something, but I did not care turn my head...not until I had my fingers round the butt of the Peacemaker.

Gradually I sneaked my hand towards it until the tips of my fingers felt the cold metal of the cylinder. But before I could get a grip, a boot came crashing down on my hand. It sent a jolt of agony up my arm and into my brain. The high cowboy heel ground into the flesh.

I moaned, and there came a kick on my head which hurled me into unconsciousness.

When I blinked open my eyes an eternity later, I discovered my hands were tied behind my back and my ankles were lashed together. The side of my face was stiff with dried blood where the skin had been sliced. Then I remembered the sharp silver spurs. I felt so sick I groaned.

'Are you all right?' came the anxious voice of Golden Dollar.

'No,' I replied honestly. 'I'm just about alive but otherwise I feel lousy. Who jumped us?'

'Two men. I think they belong to the Noon Gang. I

woke up and saw them looking down at us. One said, "That's them." Then you woke up and they hurt you.'

'What's happened to Pablo?' I asked.

'I don't know. He just wasn't there when I opened my eyes.'

'I wouldn't be surprised if the Lambs weren't in league with Joshua Noon,' I said. 'In spite of all their talk about righteousness, I'm sure New Jerusalem would make a dandy little hideout for an outlaw. Maybe he knows them of old, or maybe he stopped here on his way and left word what to do if we should come along. I guess one of the Lambs must have ridden off in the night and brought these two characters back to take care of us.'

'What will they do with us?'

I could hazard an answer but there was not much point in replying. My only surprise was that they hadn't done it already. For a while we lay in painful silence. I knew that the tight bonds round Golden Dollar's supple body must be giving her hell as they bit into the flesh.

The light was growing stronger. My head ached so much I was forced to close my eyes. I just lay like a trussed fowl, cursing myself for being caught like this.

Mentally I blamed Pablo, too, for bringing us here. He had managed to get away somehow. He would not have to pay the price for his stupidity, but we would. I felt an unreasonable bitterness towards him.

I wondered how the execution would be arranged. As the Law did not reach such a forsaken spot, it would present few problems for Noon's two desperados. Maybe they would take us a little way from New Jerusalem and fake an Indian killing. This idea made me think of my father's death. Fake Indian killings seemed to be the curse of our family.

After this morning, it would be the end of the family. I had always hoped that someday I would have a son to carry on the chain of which I was a link. In fact, I had a private dream.. .a dream of a ranch with clean white buildings and big black cattle grazing on the blue grass. In this dream world there would be no need to carry a gun any more. I could grow old pleasantly and watch my boy grow up until he was tall enough to take over.

It might have all come about if I had found the gold that was hidden at El Dedo de Dios. It would have been a certainty if my father's partner had been content with his share and had not committed murder somewhere out here in the lonely wasteland.

I felt a sudden surge of hate for Sherman when I thought of what the tragedy of his act had led to. The ironical thing was that not even he had benefited from it. Rather than help his daughter, his legacy would be the very reason for her death!

I felt so furious that I strained against my bonds, but had I been ten times as strong it would not have helped against the plaited rawhide.

Then I heard the door creak and several of the Lambs entered. Our feet were unbound and we were unceremoniously lugged to a standing position. Because of the pain as the blood started to flow in my ankles again I staggered. To encourage me to stand still a bearded youth punched me in the mouth.

'Stand straight, ye misbegotten sinner,' he cried, full of righteous indignation and courage, which may have been aided by the fact that my hands were still tied behind my back. Not to be left out of the fun, another slapped Golden Dollar across the cheek. My blood turned to ice and murder filled my heart.

I had no reason to care for this girl, yet at the sound of the blow and her choked cry I felt nothing but sheer animal hatred for those ragged bums. This feeling was followed by an unexpected wave of sympathy for her. After all, we had faced the Apaches together, and now we would be facing death together.

68

'No matter what happens to us today, you coyote,' I gritted, 'you will remember that blow someday and you will wish you had never done it.'

He was about to hit me to show he didn't care when Noon's two boys appeared.

'Hurry up there,' snapped one. 'If you holy rollers gotta have a trial you'd better hurry up. We've gotta catch up with the Boss.'

We were led out into bright sunlight. The Lambs of the Lord were standing in a big circle. They were grinning like wolves when they see a wounded steer.

At the far end of the square, made up of the paintless shacks of New Jerusalem, stood Brother Jeremiah in a set of scarlet robes. There was a mad glitter in his eye. Behind him there had been erected a crude gallows under which stood a cart with a fleabitten burro in the shafts.

We were marched up to him, then pushed down into a kneeling position on the ground. We must have looked like a couple about to be married. The Lambs closed in, while the two members of the Noon Gang watched with amused contempt. I had recognised one as Curly Roscoe, an enterprising young killer with a price on his head.

'You two worthless critters have brought sin and shame to our city of New Jerusalem,' began Brother Jeremiah in a high voice. 'You have betrayed our hospitality. You carry evil like a leper carries the plague. You have defiled our humble ways... you...'

He was really getting worked up, and loving every moment of it. When he had to stop to gulp in more air, the Lambs would get in the act with a chorus of 'Amen, amen!' or sometimes something more fancy like 'Hark unto the words of the prophet!' Finally the old goat ran out of insults.

'And just what are we supposed to have done?' I

demanded in the silence that followed. My voice did not tremble but inside I was scared as I had never been scared before. Over Brother Jeremiah's shoulder I could see the twin nooses that hung from the gallows swinging lazy-like in the faint desert breeze. And if I, who was no stranger to violent death, was feeling this way, I wondered how Golden Dollar felt in the hands of this set of lunatics who were staging this mock trial purely for their own perverted enjoyment.

'Your accusers stand behind you,' thundered the Chief Lamb. 'Speak up Mr Roscoe.'

Curly and his buddy could hardly control their laughter.

'These two outlaws are wanted for murder, stage robbery, hoss thievin', cattle rustlin' and settin' fire to churches,' chuckled Curly.

'Sure, they came to New Jerusalem plannin' to rob its peaceful an' honest citizens,' added his mate.

At this information a shout of anger went up from the Lambs.

That is enough,' Brother Jeremiah cried in a voice that plainly showed how shocked he was at our crimes. 'Often the Lambs of the Lord have been persecuted as we have crossed the land...' (This was something I could understand.) '...but at last we found our new home, our New Jerusalem. Here we will be persecuted no more by the ungodly. Therefore as the appointed leader of this flock, as the prophet of the Lord and...and...the...uh...Judge of the Temple...'

'How much are these two paying you to get us out of the way?' I demanded.

Curly Roscoe kicked me. 'You shut up until Brother Jeremiah has finished his piece,' he giggled.

'I have sifted the evidence against you two sinners, and that against your partner who slunk off in the night,' intoned the Judge of the Temple ignoring my interruption, 'and I solemnly sentence you to be hanged by the neck – and goddam you both to hell!'

The verdict was a popular one. The Lambs gave a cry of joy at this manifestation of justice and willing hands hoisted us on to the cart. I closed my eyes as I felt the rope adjusted round my neck.

Time seemed to stand still. It was as though everything was frozen. I can remember that endless moment in fine detail, and I shall until the day I die.

Side by side, Golden Dollar and I stood on the cart under the crossbar of the makeshift gallows. Before us stood the grinning Lambs, the men in front, their scrawny womenfolk a little further back. The kids were peering with wonder from round their mothers' skirts.

I was aware of the sweat trickling under my hemp collar. I guess I would have sweated just as much if it had been snowing. I knew that within seconds Brother Jeremiah would hit the burro on the rump and we would swing painfully into eternity.

'Bill, Bill,' Golden Dollar said in a tense voice. 'I just want you to know...' I never knew what she was going to say, though later on I think I knew what it might have been. As she spoke, the leader of the Lambs raised his shaft to strike the scrawny beast standing patiently in the shafts. Then everything seemed to dissolve into confusion. There was a loud report and the burro gave a grunt and sank to the ground. The cart shook, but Golden Dollar and I kept our feet.

There was another report. Curly Roscoe gave a bellow and dropped to his knees, then sprawled forward untidily. Meanwhile the Lambs milled round, trying to figure where the shots were coming from. One bullet threw up the dirt by the second outlaw. Both he and I looked round for the sharpshooter, but neither of us could spot him.

Another shot, and the outlaw, who now had a pistol

in his hand, was whirled round. Then he lay moaning beside the mortal remains of Curly Roscoe.

Suddenly a tongue of flame leapt up with a startling roar from a shack. As I watched fascinated, another shanty exploded into flame. The wood of New Jerusalem was tinder dry. Within seconds the hungry flames had spread to other dwellings.

Above the crackle of the flames, the neighing of terrified horses and the screams of the womenfolk, the crack of the unseen marksman's rifle continued.

But in the middle of the uproar Brother Jeremiah was not forgetting us. Grasping the end of the cart, he began pushing in an attempt to move it from under us. I tried to kick his white-knuckled fingers, and nearly hanged myself in the attempt. The cart rocked dangerously. Then a bullet shattered Brother Jeremiah's elbow and he went reeling away.

Now a terrified cry was going up from the Lambs: 'The vigilantes! The vigilantes!' I guess that in the past these human vultures had been raided by the vigilantes, and now they feared the self-appointed guardians of the law were upon them again. They began to melt away, running past their burning homes. Their idea was probably to lie low in the desert until the trouble was over.

So, within a minute of expecting to die, Golden Dollar and I stood looking down a deserted square. Before us were sprawled the bodies of Noon's two gunmen as well as a Lamb who had stopped a fatal bullet.

The buildings opposite the gallows were all afire and the heat caught us in the face. The first to get alight suddenly collapsed in a firework display of sparks. Into this scene of destruction I saw our rescuer appear. He stood up on the roof of the shanty in which he had spent the night. Then, rifle in hand, he jumped down and ran towards us.

'Pablo, you old son of a gun!' I yelled.

'Excuse me for being so long, *señor*,' he panted as he leapt up on the cart and began to saw through Golden Dollar's bonds with a hunting knife.

'I had to wait until the last minute because I wanted to start the shooting at the same time the shacks caught alight,' he explained. 'While you were on trial I managed to lay a trail of blasting powder. Very useful stuff, blasting powder, *señor*!'

Golden Dollar was freed. She stood on the cart rubbing her bruised wrists while Pablo went to work on me.

'Where the hell did you get blasting powder from?' I asked in amazement.

'I always carry some in my saddlebags, *señor*. Often I have used it when prospecting in the past, but not always for blowing up rocks. Hurry now, my friends. Once those loco Lambs realise they have been stampeded by one poor Mexican, they will be back...'

As soon as I was freed, we ran over to the hut where I found the Peacemaker still lying on the dirt floor. With its cool butt in my hand I felt I could face all our fanatical enemies and enjoy it. It is wonderful what confidence a .45 can give a man!

While Pablo kept watch from the roof, Golden Dollar and I hurriedly saddled up and loaded our water bags on the terrified pack animals. We could hardly see what we were doing because of the clouds of smoke that rolled from the blazing shacks. The roar of the flames had grown so loud we had to yell to make ourselves heard.

I had just secured the last water bag when Golden Dollar cried: 'Look out, Bill!'

I turned. Round the corner of the hut appeared a Lamb of the Lord, the same one who had slapped Golden Dollar earlier on. He was holding a mean-looking pitchfork, and by the expression on his face he had every intention of running me through with it.

There was not time to draw the six-shooter. I just danced to one side and managed to grab the handle of the fork as he blundered past me. Then we began a struggle, each trying to wrestle the haft free from the other. Because the rawhide had stopped my circulation at my wrists, my hands were ridiculously weak.

I felt my fingers opening even though I tried to keep them clenched tight with every ounce of will power I possessed. Suddenly my opponent gave a superhuman wrench which sent me sprawling on my back.

'Die ye accursed!' he cried in triumph. He raised the pitchfork, ready to pin me to the earth. But the expected blow never came. Golden Dollar threw a handful of sand into his face. He lunged blindly and buried the fork harmlessly in the ground a yard from me. Cursing, and still blinded, he struggled to draw it out.

I leapt to my feet and brought the butt of my gun crashing down on his thick skull. The impact sounded horrible. I had the feeling he would never be the same guy again. I reflected how quickly my words to him had come to pass.

On the roof above Pablo fired twice.

'They are returning, *señor*,' he shouted. A ragged volley emphasised his words.

'They are trying to surround us,' he added as he fired again.

'Come down, the horses are ready,' I yelled.

While he descended I sent a couple of shots whistling across the square just to make sure the Lambs kept their heads down and wouldn't get an accurate sighting on us.

Golden Dollar climbed into the saddle. Pablo and I mounted, and then, with each of us leading a pack animal, we spurred away from the blazing buildings and into the desert. Several bullets hummed uncomfortably close, but after a few minutes there was a ridge of rock between us

74

and New Jerusalem and we were safe.

'Do you think they will follow us?' asked Golden Dollar as we slowed to a canter.

'It is very doubtful, *señorita,*' answered Pablo. 'Those dogs have not the courage. They are only brave when they have some wretched traveller trapped.'

'But how did you get away in the night?' I asked.

'It was just good luck, *señor,*' he said. 'I have sharp ears, even when I sleep. I heard the sound of horses. I woke up and went out to see what it was. It must have been the arrival of Noon's men, but in the dark I could see nothing. So I scouted round the shacks. While I was doing this I heard them break in and make you prisoners. There was nothing I could do then, so I hid on the roof until dawn.

Then, while they had you on trial, I got to work with my blasting powder. They were enjoying your discomfort too much to notice me. When I lit the trail of powder I got back on the roof and began shooting.'

'Droppin' that burro was one of the prettiest pieces of gun work I've ever seen,' I said from my heart.

'God guided the bullet,' said the Mexican modestly.

We breasted another slope. Looking back we could see a distant column of smoke drifting lazily skywards.

'We have our revenge,' said Pablo. 'Still, I must make confession for taking life.'

We rode on and the pillar of smoke that marked all that was left of New Jerusalem gradually dwindled behind us.

75

CHAPTER 10

Through the rest of the day we rode into the burning Gila Desert. The further we penetrated the more harsh the scenery grew. The only patches of shade were those cast by sharp rocks and time worn boulders.

Sometimes out of the corner of our eyes we would be aware of a flash of movement as a lizard – perhaps one of those grotesque Gila monsters that gave the desert its name – would dart from one razor-edged shadow to another. The vegetation had thinned out...no more saguaros, no more sage. There was only the rare clump of mesquite or a lonely, stunted Joshua tree.

We hardly spoke to each other now.

Pablo rode ahead, his eyes searching the trembling horizon. In his hand he held a compass by which he continually checked our position. There was no trail to guide us. Our horses had to pick their way over sand and shale. Sometimes they had to scramble up slopes of pebbles that slid away under them. Often we skirted small red rock mesas which the wind had carved into fantastic shapes.

Since her ordeal early that morning Golden Dollar had said very little. I could not but admire her determination to keep going. Not once did she complain of the heat, or the thirst caused by the careful rationing of our water. Though I did not like to admit it to myself, I was gaining more and more respect for her even though she was Sherman's daughter.

It was mid-afternoon when we found ourselves crossing a fairly level plain. As it meant that our mounts need no longer go in single file, I found myself riding beside her. Pablo still rode ahead, every now and then sweeping the landscape with his telescope.

'Mr Tashlin,' she said, 'what did you think about when we were standing on that cart this morning with the ropes round our necks?'

'I was too scared to think clearly,' I admitted.

'But you must have thought of something?'

'Maybe. I had been thinking of something I was going to miss...a dream I had about a ranch in a quiet valley some place where I could forget about carrying a gun. I guess I also thought that my death would mean the end of a sort of chain that had been going on from generation to generation almost since time began.'

'Very profound thoughts for a gun-fighter, Mr Tashlin!' Seeing the look of annoyance on my face, she said quickly: 'I'm sorry. I didn't mean to be nasty. Let's keep a truce. We've been through too much together to quarrel now.'

'Sure,' I agreed. 'There's not any point in bein' childish out here on the Gila.'

'Fine,' she said. 'Once we get the gold we can split it and go our separate ways...'

'Split it?' I echoed. 'But surely it belongs to me. In that note I left you – which you didn't bother to read – I said I'd let you have a part of what I found out here, but the idea of sharing it fifty-fifty is crazy!'

'No it's not. My father found it with your father. We should share it equally...*

'Yes, but your father killed mine...'

'You have no proof of that. No one can say exactly what happened...'

'I know goddam well it was no Apache massacre,' I said stubbornly. 'Red Cloud was my father's friend. But if it was a massacre, then tell me how come your father managed to survive it?'

'How the hell do I know! I wasn't there,' she cried. 'Every one who was there is dead now. You are only guessing...'

'You know what I say is true, only you're too gosh-darned pig-headed to admit it...'

'Goddam you,' shouted Golden Dollar in a tone of voice no lady should ever use. 'That gold has warped you. Greed is making you crazy. You will twist anything, there is nothing you will not do...'

'At least I didn't become a dancehall tramp to get at it,' I interrupted.

There was a flash of hatred in her eyes as she spurred her horse and rode ahead of me. Our truce had not lasted very long.

Just before nightfall we halted to make camp. Precious water was given to the horses in a canvas bucket. Their tongues rasped against the rough bottom long after it was dry.

Shadows raced across the plain as the sun slipped below the edge of the world. Suddenly it was night, a gentle night spangled with stars. I lounged against a slab of rock that was gradually cooling after the baking it had received during the day. Pablo was making a tiny fire out of greasewood sticks. It was a clever fire, so arranged that there was hardly a flame visible. It was obvious he had learned the art from the Indians. Soon the smell of coffee wafted towards me.

Golden Dollar was pointedly refusing to talk to me, so to cover the awkward silence Pablo chatted away good-naturedly while he made supper.

'I must say that tonight I shall enjoy sleeping out with the knowledge that the citizens of New Jerusalem will be doing the same after my little fire this morning,' he chuckled. 'I have done plenty of funny things in the past, but I have never burned down a settlement before.'

'It was some blaze,' I agreed. 'But I wonder what

Joshua Noon'll think when his two men don't turn up.'

'It does not matter, *señor*. By tomorrow's light, if God is willing, we shall see El Dedo de Dios.'

'Yeah, but I hope we won't find he's got there before us.'

'There is little chance. We have come by a very direct route, and we have pushed our horses. Joshua Noon is a stranger to the Gila and he cannot move as fast as us with his mules. Anyway, by midday tomorrow it will all be clear.'

After we had finished our supper of beans, and cleaned our tin plates by rubbing them with sand, Golden Dollar and Pablo wrapped themselves in their blankets and were soon asleep. For a while I lay looking up at the stars above my head. I wondered if tomorrow would bring what I had searched for so long. Then I too drifted off into sleep with my hand clasped round the butt of the Peacemaker.

I woke at dawn. Just for a few minutes before the sun hoisted itself over the horizon the desert was a place of beauty, then everything seemed to change into a hell on earth. One could feel the wave of heat come with the sun almost as though a great furnace door had been opened. The stark light glittered on the mica particles in the sand so that you had to screw up your eyes. You suddenly began sweating, but your sweat dried almost instantly leaving whitish salt marks on your shirt. The very air burnt your nostrils and made your throat into a parched tube.

This was the real, terrible Gila. There was not a hint of green anywhere, only the monotonous colours of sand and rock. There was not even the whitening skull of a steer because nothing living dared venture this far into such a dangerous wasteland.

Without a word we saddled up. I guessed that each of us was privately dreading the ordeal that we knew lay ahead. It was only the thought of my father's gold that drove me on.

The hot silence, the sense of brooding death and the knowledge that our water was low would have been enough to warn off a sane man, but I doubt if I was sane. I had gold fever just as badly as any old crazy coot of a prospector who spends his life in desolate places hoping day after day, year after year, that he is going to strike a bonanza. We came to the top of a rise. Pablo halted and turned to us.

'There is it, amigos. El Dedo de Dios – the Finger of God!' He pointed to the west where a pinnacle of rock stood lonely on the horizon. But even from this distance it looked like a finger pointing straight up at the heavens. It began as a mesa, which gave it the appearance of a knuckle, then became one of those freak pillars of sandstone that nature sometimes carves in the badlands.

'So, that is where the treasure is,' I said, feeling a certain awe. 'But the trouble is that while it is a dandy landmark, we still have to find where the gold is stashed away.'

'It must be on the pinnacle itself,' said Golden Dollar. 'I remember my father saying in his letter that he had hidden it at the tip of the finger.'

'But how the heck could he get the gold up there,' I said. 'There was more than a man could carry remember.'

'We'll know soon enough,' said Pablo. 'Let us not waste time here.'

His words were followed by a high insect whine above our head, followed by a faint report. We turned in our saddles to see where the shot had come from. From the vantage point of the ridge I could make out a line of dots to the north-east. I borrowed Pablo's telescope and in its circle I was able to see that these dots were horsemen and mules moving slowly over the face of the desert. By focussing carefully I was able to see that the leading rider was Joshua Noon.

Obviously they had spotted us silhouetted on the ridge. Even as I watched I saw the man next to Noon raise his long-barrelled rifle and aim in our direction.

'We'd better not hang around,' I snapped as its bullet whistled harmlessly overhead. I led the way down the opposite side of the ridge.

'What are we going to do now?' asked Golden Dollar, her face a picture of dismay.

'We are going to carry on to El Dedo de Dios,' I said. 'We are at least an hour ahead of those coyotes.,.'

'Senor, I know how you must feel,' said Pablo, 'but an hour is not enough. Even if we find the gold in that time, there would not be enough time to load it on to our horses. Remember they are ten heavily armed and desperate men. Let us turn back while there is still time, *señor*.'

The heat, the disappointment and the fear of the murderous Noon Gang was suddenly too much for my self-control. The gold fever that had burned in my blood suddenly gripped me and made me explode with anger.

'You speak like a coward, Mexican,' I snarled. 'Leave, if you want to...but I am gonna find that treasure if it's the last thing I do.'

'That could well be, *señor*,' said Pablo very quietly. 'But I said I would guide you to El Dedo de Dios and if you want to gamble your life, then I must too. Come, we have little time.'

As we spurred our horses I saw Golden Dollar looking at me with contempt, and my anger turned to shame. I had called Pablo a coward even though he had risked his life to save us single-handed at New Jerusalem!

81

CHAPTER 11

It was a crazy ride across the desert. Having seen El Dedo de Dios on the horizon, I was fooled into thinking we were close to it. Now, as I ran the rowels of my spurs over the flanks of my panting horse, I began to realise it was much further away than I'd thought.

Though we had ridden hard for a couple of hours, the slender column on the far edge of the desert hardly increased in size. It appeared to writhe and dance in the tortured air of the Gila. Sometimes I feared it was just a mirage.

Pablo's words kept coming back to me. How the hell could I ever hope to locate the gold before Joshua Noon and his gang arrived on the scene? At the most it would take them a couple of hours to catch up with us, maybe less, and it might take days to find the hiding place of the treasure.

I felt furious with myself as we rode on. It seemed that everything I had done was wrong, including the insulting of Pablo Martinez. Yet there was nothing I could do about it. I just hoped for some miracle to happen when we reached El Dedo which would give me the gold and let us get away from our enemies.

'We must have a halt, *señor*,' said Pablo finally. The horses need a few minutes rest. If we are to reach El Dedo, we must give them water.'

I was about to argue, but deep down I knew he was right so I kept quiet. We dismounted in a gulley and I poured water from our dwindling supply into the canvas bucket.

When we had started out from Tombstone our horses had been healthy animals but now their bones appeared ready to poke through their hides.

We gulped down some water ourselves. It was warm and tasted bad, but to us it was better than the most expensive champagne money could buy. I noticed Pablo looking at the amount of water that remained in the skins on our pack animals...and I knew the thoughts that were going through his mind. Even if we set back now there was hardly enough to see us back to civilisation. Had our departure from New Jerusalem been more friendly and dignified we could have filled up there, but when we left half our containers were empty.

We sat silent in the shade of a rock and Pablo and I smoked a cigarette each. I wanted to say something to him to make things right after my outburst of anger, but something held me back. I found I could not apologise in front of Golden Dollar, and this made me feel even worse. Why the hell should I worry what this dancehall girl, the daughter of a murderer, thought! It was not as though I was in love with her! In fact, apart from when we had shared a sort of comradeship in the face of danger, my feelings were exactly the opposite.

I finished the smoke and hauled myself painfully to my feet. I could stand this tension no longer. I needed action.

'Let's get cracking,' I said. 'These cayuses don't need any more rest. I'll bet the Noon Gang ain't resting theirs.'

We mounted and rode out of the gulch. Sometimes Pablo would turn in his saddle and sweep the terrain behind us with his Navy telescope, but there was no sign of the Noon Gang. The desert was now so undulating that even if they were a few hundred yards behind us it would have been doubtful if we could spot them.

By midday the stone finger ahead seemed to

suddenly increase in size as we approached it. There was the magic of an optical illusion about the way it suddenly began to dwarf us. I saw now that while it was broad at the base, as it went higher its walls became almost vertical. I also noticed that the top of it split into two peaks which, from the angle we were approaching, were separated by a slash of blue sky. One seemed to be slightly higher than the other.

'El Dedo is sacred to the Apaches,' said Pablo. 'Some times the medicine men go to the top of the taller peak and talk to the Great Spirit.'

'How the heck do they get up there?' I asked.

'There is a path. It is many years since I was here, but I remember that it winds round and round the pinnacle. Parts of it were cut by the Indians long ago. Perhaps it has crumbled away now.'

An hour later we were urging our swaying mounts up the slope that led up to the red sandstone walls of El Dedo. Pablo, who from this elevated position was using his telescope again, grunted and handed me the instrument. In the circle of the glass I once more saw the dots which I knew to be the Noon Gang.

'They're still a mighty long way behind us,' I said, trying to sound cheerful.

'Si, señor,' said Pablo. 'You have about an hour to find your treasure...'

'Maybe that'll be plenty,' I replied. 'Let's circle El Dedo and find this path you were telling me about.'

We began to ride round the towering walls of the pinnacle. Sometimes they rose straight up from the desert like cliffs rise from the sea, but in other parts rockfalls had created gentler slopes. It was above one of these ancient mounts that I glimpsed what seemed to be a bridle track.

'That's it, señor,' Pablo exclaimed in excitement. 'It twists round and round El Dedo until it reaches the twin peaks.'

'Okay,' I said dismounting. 'You wait here with the horses. 'I'm going up.' I tossed him the reins and began scrambling up the rubble to the point where the path began. It was narrow and worn, but I felt a sure-footed mule could be led up it. Maybe that was how Sherman had got the gold to the top... supposing there was gold at the top!

As I followed the path as fast as I could, with rock fragments clattering into space with every step, Golden Dollar suddenly shouted 'Wait!' and began to scramble after me.

But I did not wait. Nothing was going to hinder me now. Looking back on it, it was a crazy setup. There was Golden Dollar and I racing up this giddy track while down below Pablo held the horses and probably wondered how long it would be before we were dodging the Noon gang's bullets!

At last I reached the point where the pillar forked. The path came round the side of the smaller peak, crossed a dizzy ridge of rock only a couple of feet wide and then continued to spiral the other. Walking this natural bridge was not a pleasant experience. It was about thirty feet long and, with a terrifying drop on either side, it was almost like walking a tightrope. Somehow I made it to the second spire, and then paused to look back at Golden Dollar. She was halfway across and standing perfectly still. I realised she was frozen with terror.

Muttering a curse, I edged out, grasped her hand and led her over.

'Thank you,' she said sullenly. 'I guess I never did have a head for heights.'

Together we continued up the final stretch. I noticed that here and there steps had been hewn out of the rock where the natural path petered out. At last we reached a dozen time-worn steps. We panted up those – and found ourselves on the very summit of El Dedo de

Dios.

It was composed of a flat plateau of about twenty square yards with a great slab of rock rearing up at the northern edge. To the east, about sixty feet away and a little lower, was the rock-strewn summit of the other peak. But what interested me was a shallow cave that the wind had carved in the northern mass of rock. Its opening was only about four feet high, and it was doubtful if it was even that much deep. It was hard to tell because, with the sun still high, its interior was in the deepest shadow.

Golden Dollar and I walked over to the floor of eroded sandstone to it. At first I could see nothing in the blackness, then I made out something white. As my eyes adjusted I saw it was the skull of a mule. Behind it was a litter of bleached bones...and something that glinted yellow.

Sure enough, it was a tiny gleam of gold. I crept forward on hands and knees and found a pile of leather sacks. The dry heat had made the leather brittle and in parts it had split, allowing gold dust and nuggets to spill out.

'So this is it,' breathed Golden Dollar, 'this is what we have come all this way to find.'

'Yeah. Your father's directions were dead right. He must have brought those leather saddlebags up here by mule, and then killed it. Or maybe it just died. But it was a brilliant place to hide it. Even the Indians would keep away because this is a sacred rock. Only medicine men can come here, and then only once in a generation.'

'Poor Dad,' murmured Golden Dollar.

I was about to make some stinging retort because here was the final piece of evidence that Sherman had murdered his comrades, but I stifled the remark. What was the point of quarrelling again. But I knew that if there really had been an Indian massacre no one would have been able to lead a heavily laden mule up and down the

86

pinnacle.

Suddenly I was weary. It was as though a spring inside me had suddenly uncoiled. The past was dead. I could not hate Sherman any more. Nor could I even dislike his daughter. She was not responsible for the past.

'Come,' I muttered, breaking the silence. 'The gang must be gettin' close.'

'But what are we going to do with it, now we have found it?'

'I know one thing,' I said grimly. 'I don't aim to let Joshua Noon get his thievin' hands on it.'

Golden Dollar sighed. 'I expected you to say that, but how are you going to stop him?'

'Up here a man with a rifle could hold back an army,' I said vaguely.

'Until his water runs out, or he goes to sleep and the enemy sneaks across I the ridge,' she said. 'Besides, the sun would burn him to death on this exposed chunk of rock. We wouldn't last a day.'

'What d'you mean – we? I ain't askin' you to stay here. I'll hold 'em off an you can go with Pablo to get help...'

'...and leave you with all this gold! You must be crazy, Bill Tashlin. Half of it's mine and I aim to keep my eye on it.'

'I couldn't get very far with this lot, even if the Noon Gang would let me,' I snapped. 'Have some common-sense, woman!'

But she wasn't listening. She was looking at some small nuggets she had placed in her palm.

'Look at this gold, Bill Tashlin,' she said softly. 'See it shine in the sun. Don't you realise that on this rock there is enough to buy ranches, or travel the world, or do anything we like.' It was as though the precious pebbles had hypnotised her.

'This is the end of a long journey for us both,' she

whispered.

'Or maybe the beginning,' I found myself saying. I put my arms round her and turned her towards me. For a second I was aware of her eyes looking searchingly into my face, then our dry, desert-cracked lips met and I realised I had found a second treasure on the summit of El Dedo de Dios.

* * *

It was the sound of a spur striking against stone that made me turn. Over the edge of our tiny plateau appeared a sombrero, then the sweat-glistening face of Pablo beneath it.

'*Nombre de Dios*!' he exclaimed. 'Have you forgotten the gang approaches! What...' And then his eyes caught the glitter of the gold in the shadow of the recess. For a moment he could not speak. Then he said softly: 'So you have found it. It is real. I believed it was just a loco legend, a desert myth. But it is real, and there is enough to make a man many times rich.'

'You're dead right, my friend,' I laughed. 'And don't worry – we'll see you are rich, too. Now listen to me. I am going to stay up here. I can hold off the Noon Gang. Meanwhile you go and get help. Go back to Nogales. I'm sure Captain Marvin Dexter of the cavalry would come to the rescue again. I think he had a weakness for golden hair.'

Golden Dollar laughed at my jibe. And it was a happy laugh!

'But I cannot leave you alone, *señor*,' said Pablo. 'Sure, you could hold off many men up here, but what about when you sleep?'

'I shall stay with him,' Golden Dollar said. 'We've fought Indians together, so I guess we can manage the Noon Gang together.'

'All right,' said Pablo. 'Then we must hurry. Come down to the horses and get all the supplies you need.'

Without another word he led the way down the steps, across the bridge between the twin peaks and down the spiralling path to the rock-strewn sand below.

The horses were tethered to some boulders. I unsheathed my Winchester and grabbed a full water skin.

'Take everything you want,' said Pablo. 'I shall travel light. All I want is some water.'

There's precious little of that,' I said. 'But be sure you take what you need. You're the most important man in this operation.'

'What about the horses?' asked Golden Dollar as she started up the track with a bag of provisions.

'I shall shoot them,' Pablo said.

'Oh no.'

'Senorita, it is not a job I like. But a quick unexpected death is better than a slow one by thirst.'

Pablo was right. He was a man of the desert and he knew that at times he had to be as ruthless as the desert itself.

'You carry on up,' I told Golden Dollar. 'I'll join you in a few minutes.'

'Let's get it over, *señor*,' said Pablo when she was out of sight. He drew his revolver. I turned and began to pack some .44 rifle ammunition into a gunny sack. I can't stand seeing a horse die.

Pablo's gun crashed again and again, sending echoes flying from the red walls of El Dedo. Then there was silence.

'Adios, amigo,' he said swinging himself into the saddle of the remaining horse which was twitching with terror.

'Adios, amigo,' said I. 'And please forget what I said earlier today.'

'I have forgotten already, *señor*. Things said in the desert often mean nothing.'

With the waterskin over my shoulder the

Winchester and the gunny sack in my hands, I began the dizzy climb for the second time. I must have been a couple of hundred feet up when I heard the shot. I looked down, but being on the north side of the pillar I could see nothing but empty desert. There came another shot. It was the dull boom of a buffalo gun. I scrambled upwards, wondering what the hell had happened to Pablo.

I saw everything when I reached the rock bridge. Pablo was galloping towards the west. To the south the Noon Gang had spread out and were trying to head him off. For a moment it seemed as though he would outdistance them, but then I saw that Joshua Noon had dismounted and was taking careful aim at the retreating figure. Before I could aim the Winchester at him his buffalo gun thundered again. To my horror I saw Pablo's horse plunge headlong, throwing up a fountain of sand. As Pablo staggered to his feet the riders began to close in.

I was surprised they were not using their guns on him. Then I realised they probably wanted him for a hostage. No doubt by threatening to torture him, they thought they could force us to give up our vantage point.

But they still had to catch him, and Pablo was now running towards the base of El Dedo. I swung my sights on to the nearest horseman. I squeezed the trigger. Sand spurted a yard in front of the horse's hooves. It threw its rider as it reared in terror.

I worked the lever and fired again and again. My bullets were enough to halt the rest of the gang. For a moment they seemed uncertain where they were coming from, then they saw me silhouetted high against the sky. Slugs began to splatter on the rock beneath my feet.

At least I had managed to draw their attention from Pablo for a few seconds. I took careful aim at another member of the gang. Again I had the strange feeling of knowing that I would hit him, even though he was a tiny target. My uncanny presentiment was right. His scream

90

came faintly to my ears. He slumped forward over his mount's neck.

The others turned and galloped back with my bullets whining after them. There was no doubt I had the advantage and they weren't going to take any more chances.

Meanwhile Pablo was out of my line of sight. I prayed that he would not be picked off as he climbed the track up the finger. The Noon Gang had now divided. One group was taking the horses out of range of my Winchester while the remainder had taken cover behind rocks and boulders and were doing their best to perforate me.

Suddenly I saw Pablo stagger round the corner of the lesser peak. His side was red with blood and he moved like a drunkard. I edged across the bridge to l him. As I got closer I saw that his face was deathly white under his swarthy tan. Under one arm he carried a blood-spotted bundle which he clung to with the same determination as a child clutching its favourite toy.

It was a nightmare journey back to the summit of the finger. Bullets whistled about us as I fought to stop Pablo falling off into space.

By some miracle we reached the tiny plateau where, by keeping down, we were safe from the guns of the Noon Gang. Pablo collapsed in the scanty shade of the treasure cave. Golden Dollar bent over him, tearing away his shirt to dress the wound on his left side. The bullet had entered the flesh and glanced off one of the lower ribs. A painful wound, but at least not dangerous provided no infection set in.

Cautiously I looked over the edge of the plateau. The only sign of the conflict was Pablo's dead horse. Noon's boys were behind the scattered rock outcrops, no doubt waiting impatiently for thirst to accomplish what their guns had failed to do.

CHAPTER 12

Pablo Martinez groaned in his sleep. Golden Dollar and I lay in a strange world of shadows on the top of El Dedo de Dios. The night breeze whispered eerily round us. I cuddled the stock of the Winchester, keeping the barrel trained on the moonlit ridge of rock that joined the twin peaks. If we were to be attacked, I knew our enemies would have to cross it.

Sometimes the silver light played tricks on my weary eyes. Once I was sure I saw a figure move in a shadow at the opposite end of the ridge. I fired, but my bullet merely ricocheted off sandstone.

As the night wore on, I would doze off for seconds or minutes at a time, then wake in a panic half expecting to see lithe figures moving towards our peak for a surprise attack. I could not master this desperate urge to sleep. My eyes were red with fatigue and my body was aching for rest...

Some sixth sense roused me. As I blinked my eyelids open, I saw the shadow of a man between me and the stars. With relief I recognised it as the bulky shape of Pablo.

'It's all right, *señor*,' he whispered. 'I keep watch.'

'But you're wounded.'

'I get better quick. What worries me, *señor*, is that we could be attacked when we are off our guard. As we get more exhausted, and more thirsty, it is more likely to happen. I do not wish to speak of such things in front of the *señorita*, but we both know, *señor*, that soon we will be in a very bad way.'

'You're goddam right,' I agreed. 'Noon can either wait for us to go loco with the heat an' thirst, or, if he hasn't got enough water to last out that long, he can sneak up on us in the dark.'

'Si, *señor*, but I plan to make the sneaking up more difficult.'

'How?'

'I have explosive in that bag I brought up with me. If I could blow up part of that ridge between the two peaks down there, it would make it almost impossible for anyone to cross. As soon as it gets light enough I'll blast a gap in it.'

'No. I'll go. You're not in a fit condition with that wound.'

'Excuse, but have you experience with explosive, *señor*?'

I had to admit that I had not.

'Then it is a job for me. I think if they're going to attack they'll wait for enough light to see their way up El Dedo. It'd be a hard climb to come in the dark. If they come, it'll be with the dawn. I must do my work before they arrive.'

As the minutes passed, the stars in the east faded. The darkness began to turn to grey. Beside me Pablo was working with a length of fuse and his blasting charge.

'What's happening?' asked Golden Dollar, waking from a troubled sleep.

'Pablo is gonna cut the line of attack,' I answered. 'It's lucky he always happens to carry explosive in his gear.'

Pablo chuckled, then winced as a spasm of pain reminded him of his wounded side.

'Always in the desert I carry explosive,' he said. 'Remember how useful the blasting powder was for setting fire to New Jerusalem. Sometimes I use it for blasting rock to see if there is a vein of gold, sometimes it is a useful weapon against one's enemies.'

'It's getting light,' Golden Dollar said.

'Si, *señorita*. I shall go down now. Please keep me covered, *señor*. It would be unpleasant if Joshua Noon came along while I am on the ridge.'

'Don't worry,' I murmured, looking down the Winchester's barrel. Carefully the Mexican heaved his bulk over the edge of the plateau. For a while he was out of sight, then I made him out edging out on to the ridge. He was a vague shadow in a world of vague shadows.

Suddenly there was a noise. A dark figure appeared round the shoulder of the rock opposite Pablo. There was an orange stab of flame, a deep grunt from Pablo and a crack from my rifle. My shot was followed by a shriek. The dark shape went whirling over the edge of the path. But Pablo was hit. I could just make him out, lying prone along the narrow ridge. From somewhere in the shadows a fusillade of shots whined in my direction.

I pushed Golden Dollar flat and ducked my head. A terrible silence followed.

Here we were, face to face with our enemies with Pablo wounded on the ridge between us. Then, from the opposite peak came the voice of Joshua Noon, 'I'm gonna give you a chance, Tashlin.' His voice set off weird echoes. 'We can pick off your buddy any time we like now. But if you throw down your guns we'll give you a safe passage. All we want is the gold, but maybe we'll even give you a nugget to cover expenses. How's about that for a deal?' He laughed coldly. 'Now, I'm gonna give you a minute by my watch to make up your mind. In sixty seconds we'll blast your friend into Kingdom Come.'

'What can we do?' whispered Golden Dollar. 'I don't trust them. They'd probably shoot us down as soon as we appeared...'

'I guess you're right,' I said. 'But I can't leave Pablo there.'

Below I could hear him coughing. Then he began to speak, painfully.

'Señor...! – I am hurt bad. Don't – don't listen...it makes no difference... now...'

As the light grew stronger I could see him sprawled out. One hand still held a long fuse, the other his charge of explosive. He was moving weakly, but I could not make out what he was trying to do.

'Only a few more seconds, Tashlin,' yelled Noon across the gap.

I heard Pablo mutter something in Spanish. It could have been a prayer. Then I stood up.

'Okay,' I said. 'You win.'

But as I spoke I heard a faint sizzling. Looking down I saw a spark dancing round Pablo's hand.

I hurled myself flat. Next second there was a shattering concussion and a great tongue of flame shot skywards. El Dedo seemed to tremble and fragments from the blast clattered about us like painful hail.

Now I knew what Pablo had been endeavouring to do as he lay on the ridge – he had been trying to light the fuse!

Cautiously I peered over the edge. Where Pablo had lain there was a huge smoking gap. It was as though a giant's axe had crashed down on the rock bridge.

'My God,' murmured Golden Dollar. 'What a man!'

'He was a very brave Mexican,' I said.

There was nothing else to say. Thanks to Pablo Martinez there was hardly any chance of us being taken by surprise now. If anyone wanted to cross they would probably have to build some sort of a bridge.

There was the familiar sound of a shot. A bullet left a snail's trail of hot silver on a rock close to my head. I jerked it down out of the line of fire. Obviously one of Noon's boys was firing from behind the rocks on top of the opposite peak.

'Don't get the notion that this hole in the ridge is gonna stop us, Tashlin,' yelled Joshua Noon. 'We'll keep you pinned down on top of your rock, an' if my boys don't get you – the sun will. Soon you'll both be fryin' like eggs in a frypan while me an' the boys sit down below in the shade, drinkin' sweet water and figuring how we're gonna spend the gold. Meanwhile, if you are careless enough to show your heads, Bronco will take great pleasure in ventilatin' 'em. C'mon boys.'

He must have led the rest of the gang back down the path. I raised myself up to take a shot at them, but as soon as my hat appeared over the rim of the plateau Bronco neatly put a hole through the crown.

'Do that again, Tashlin,' he shouted across the gap that separated us. 'Why drag it out, man? It's gonna be a hot day, so why not get it over with!'

Golden Dollar and I lay side by side in the centre of the flat summit of the finger. It was a stalemate. In this position they couldn't get us. On the other hand, they had us trapped completely.

'It seems pretty hopeless,' said Golden Dollar. 'We're just about out of water. If we stand up we'll be shot to pieces.'

'It seems that way,' I agreed. 'And yet...well, you never know, I knew a padre once who used to say: "There's hope in the ocean, but none in the grave." We ain't dead yet, my girl. Something may turn up.'

The sun was climbing and already the heat was bringing a sheen of sweat to our faces. I made Golden Dollar lay with her head on the bags of gold in the cave. This way she got all the shade there was on El Dedo. We had half a tin mug of water each, and then there was nothing to do but wait.

Over on his peak Bronco was talkative. Obviously he was a guy who didn't relish solitude.

'Is there much gold over there?' he shouted conversationally.

'Sure is,' I yelled back. 'But you'll never see it. I'd chuck it over the side first.'

'Aw shucks, Tashlin, don't be like that. Let's do a deal, man. Stand up and throw down your guns an' we'll all share it between us like gentlemen.'

'Okay,' I said after a long pause. 'I guess I know when I'm licked...'

I winked at Golden Dollar who was looking at me as though I had gone loco.

'I'm gonna trust you, Bronco,' I said. 'I'll stand up slow like, so you don't get nervous and shoot me by accident. Okay?'

'Okay, man.'

I put my sombrero on the end of the Winchester barrel and gently raised it above the edge of the plateau. Immediately Bronco's gun barked and my hat went spinning.

'Bronco,' I said sadly. 'You ain't no gentleman.' He laughed, realising the trick I had played.

'You're plum right, Tashlin,' he cried. 'I guess I was raised bad. Ain't my fault. My pappy was a rustler and my mammy ran a sportin' house. I just never had a chance.'

'And you ain't gonna get one,' I said. 'I'll get you, Bronco, one way or another.'

An hour crawled by. Sometimes, for the want of something better to do, Bronco would send a bullet whistling over our heads, but provided we kept flat we knew that we were safe.

'Gettin' thirsty?' he inquired. 'Terrible thing, thirst. Saw a guy what died of it one time. His tongue was black an' hanging out. Oh, sorry ma'am. Forgot there was a lady present...'

'That'll do, Bronco,' I yelled furiously.

'Certainly, Mr Tashlin, sir,' he sneered. 'Anythin' you say...'

'Got a mirror?' I hissed to Golden Dollar. She nodded and produced a tiny vanity case from her pocket. By careful manoeuvring I was able to raise it and survey my enemy without him noticing.

I saw him clearly framed in the small oval of the glass. His head was visible over his rifle barrel. He was smoking and he seemed to be bored. He was not even looking in our direction, but gazing at the wraith of smoke from his cigarette.

'Listen, Golden Dollar,' I whispered. 'When I say the word I want you to toss the tin mug over the edge.'

'What are you going to do?'

'You'll see. All ready?' She nodded. I had the Peacemaker in my hand. Once more I looked at Bronco reflected in the mirror. Now he was mopping his face with his kerchief. I tried to memorise his exact position.

'Now!' I said. The tin made a hell of a noise as it bounced down the side of the pinnacle. Immediately I jumped to my feet, fired my Colt and threw myself flat again. In that second I had had a brief vision of Bronco looking in the direction of the sound of the mug.

'Did you get him?' asked Golden Dollar.

'I dunno,' I replied. 'He's probably lyin' doggo, waitin' for me to stand up again to see if I was lucky or not.'

Minutes passed. Then I heard the sound of men toiling up the steep path. There were two of them, both cursing the heat and the climb. I guessed they had come to take over the watch.

'Hey, Bronco!' one called. Then 'Goddam! Look at Bronco!'

'Right between the eyes,' said the other in a funny sort of voice. 'By Gawd, that Tashlin will pay for this. That's three of our boys he's killed.'

'No wonder he was a top gunfighter,' said the first. 'He's a natural born killer.'

The elation of having settled the score with Bronco was suddenly dulled by these remarks. This was how the world saw me – a natural born killer! Was this how Golden Dollar saw me?

I looked at her but she smiled. When I say 'smiled', I mean she drew back her cracked lips in what was meant to be a smile. It appeared more like a snarl.

'I know what you're thinking,' she said. 'But I don't think that of you.'

'My reputation began as an accident,' I said. 'I got mixed up in a fight with a stranger in a saloon a long time ago. I was just a kid and he was cheatin' me at cards. Well, I dropped him. What I didn't know was that he was a top gunman. After that... well, other things followed. One of his buddies tried to get me, but again I was lucky – and I was lucky because I was good with a gun. And so my reputation grew. Then guys would pick on me...like that kid in Las Cruces...'

'You don't need to explain,' said Golden Dollar. 'I had the same experience over Margarita.'

Time dragged on. The heat made my head swim. Sometimes I seemed to be drifting in a nightmarish world, a world of distorted shapes and fantasies born of delirium. Sometimes I forgot about the enemy, about the gold and even Golden Dollar.

I came to once and heard her whimpering like a child. I squirmed across the hot rock to her. I reached for the waterskin. It was frighteningly light. I just wet my kerchief and held it to her lips. Then I crawled back to my position with the Winchester. I made the mistake of touching the breech. The metal was so hot it raised a blister.

After that my memories were vague. At one time I had a sort of dream in which I was swimming in a pool with a waterfall splashing all over me, but when I opened my mouth and tried to drink it vanished and I was back on the hellish summit of El Dedo de Dios.

CHAPTER 13

Next morning we were awakened by the voice of Joshua Noon calling from the opposite peak: 'It's gonna be another hot day, Tashlin. I don't expect you'll last it out. You'll probably go loco and jump over the edge...'

I poked up my sombrero and, as a matter of course, a bullet whistled through it. Then Golden Dollar and I shared the last of our water. During the morning I used the little mirror sometimes to see what the enemy were up to but all I could see was the gleam of a gun barrel. After the demise of Bronco they were taking more care.

By noon I had the horrible sensation of my tongue starting to swell. I also had the strange notion that the whole world was going to tip right over. I must have moaned or something, because the next thing I remember was Golden Dollar bending over me wiping my face. Over her shoulder I could see some black dots high above. Buzzards.

In trying to help me she must have raised herself above the skyline because there was a shot and her left sleeve began to turn red.

I pulled her down and ripped open the dress where the bullet had cut a deep groove across the skin. It was painful and I had difficulty in stopping the bleeding. But she was so low that the wound did not bother her very much, she was just irritated by it. After a while she said: 'I guess this is it, isn't it, Bill?'

'Maybe,' I said.

'I think it is,' she said. 'We can't last out much longer up here. Sometimes I think I'm going crazy. A little while ago I could have sworn I saw my mother... she was walking through the sky/

Thirst gives you delusions,' I said. And I couldn't think of anything else to say.

'Well, I guess it's unimportant,' she continued. 'So a dancehall girl and a gunfighter get what's coming to them on top of a rock. So what? The world will go on just the same...just the same.. .just the same...'

Her voice became an indistinct mumble. I hoped she wouldn't come round again. I began to consider getting it over with. Life had become pure agony. Surely it was better to stand up and shoot it out like a man rather than go loco lying on my belly. But what about Golden Dollar? I couldn't leave her to the mercy of the gang.

I had heard of settlers coming West who, when hopelessly outnumbered by Indians, shot their womenfolk rather than have them captured. Maybe it was true, maybe it was just a legend...but I found myself thinking about it more and more.

A little relief came at sundown when the temperature dropped. For a while it was bearable, but it continued to drop and soon I was shivering like I had fever.

From somewhere below there came snatches of song and laughter. Apparently the Noon boys had liquid refreshment other than water. No doubt they expected to collect the gold on the next day and they were already celebrating.

Just to let them know I was still around I crept to the edge of the plateau and fired all cylinders of the Peacemaker wildly into the night.

They fired back, equally wildly. Then the sentry on the other peak sent bullets whistling through the dark and I had enough sense left to lay on my back. I looked straight up at the stars and wondered what it would be like to die.

* * *

When unwelcome consciousness returned in the morning my eyelids were so swollen I had to prise them apart with my fingers. Around the edge of the plateau I saw about a dozen black shapes – the hunched, patient shapes of buzzards. I picked up the Peacemaker with both hands, aimed at one and just managed to pull the trigger. The evil bird exploded in a cloud of black feathers. The others rose with a great beating of wings.

'So, you're still alive?' came a voice from the other peak. 'Why don't you hurry up and die so we can get out of this goddamn place.'

Then I had an idea. I had mentioned it before to the late Bronco, but now I remembered it again and it seemed one of the best ideas I'd ever had. If I crawled over to the recess I might be able to get the gold out of the old leather bags. Then I could take it, bit by bit, and throw it over the edge. That way a hell of a lot would be lost in the sand. If I couldn't have it, at least this would stop Joshua Noon and his bunch getting it.

I began to move towards the shallow cave. I was careful not to disturb Golden Dollar who seemed to be in a coma. I began to struggle to open the first bag, but my hands seemed too weak. Then I realised that somewhere guns were being fired. There was another sound, too. It was one I had heard recently but I couldn't place it.

Golden Dollar stirred and moaned. The shots continued. There was a confused shouting down below. It began to sink into my fuddled brain that the shots were not coming at us.

I crawled to the edge of the plateau and looked over, and suddenly it all became clear. A war party of Indians was advancing towards El Dedo de Dios. The Noon Gang were firing back at them from the rocks at the base of the pinnacle.

Noon was trapped, just as he had trapped us. The

idea of it made me shake with crazy laughter.

Across on the other peak Noon's sentry, a desperado called Smiler Storms, was busy firing down at the advancing Apaches.

'How about a truce, Tashlin,' he shouted over to me. 'We're both white men. You won't stand a chance if they get you.'

'Go to hell, Smiler,' I said. 'I'll shoot anyone I can, paleface or Indian.'

Below the war party was still advancing. There were about sixty braves and most of them seemed to be armed with rifles. I knew it would be just a matter of time before they had the scalps of the Noon Gang.

Then I saw a movement on the desert face. Two riders were galloping to the north-west. I could not recognise them properly until I focussed Pablo's telescope. The leading rider was Joshua Noon, followed by one of his henchmen.

Several Apaches detached themselves from the main body and gave chase. Soon all the riders were hidden from my view by the rock slab at the northern side of the plateau.

I turned to see how the battle was going below. It seemed the Indians had drawn back, leaving a couple of their number dead. Now they were milling round in a shallow gulley which protected them from the Noon Gang's bullets.

'What are they going to do?'

I turned my head to see Golden Dollar beside me.

'They'll probably charge what's left of the Noon outfit.'

'It'll only make things worse for us,' she said with a shudder.

'Well, that's the penalty for being intruders,' I said, watching the braves as they began to slither from cover to cover towards the outlaws below us.

'What do you mean?'

'I was just thinkin' of what the Indians used to tell me when I was a kid playin' round my father's tradin' post,' I said. 'The Apaches believe their ancient ancestors used to live underground. One day they climbed to the surface of the earth on a ladder made of sunbeams...'

'Like a fairy tale,' she commented

'In a way,' I agreed. 'Only they believe it as real. They think that when they reached the surface of the earth they wandered the land in great sweeping clockwise circles. Some grew tired and settled, and these became the other tribes. But the true people – the Apaches – went on and on until they reached the very centre of the world, and here they stopped...'

From below came a blood curdling war whoop. At this signal the braves leapt to their feet and charged. The defending shots became fewer and fewer. Then there was a silence, broken only by a brief scream that even at such a distance turned my stomach.

'Well, I guess that is the end of the Noon Gang,' I said. 'Apart from Smiler over there.'

'Maybe they'll go away and not notice us,' said Golden Dollar.

'I doubt it. Smiler was blazing away at them so they'll come up and get him ...then us. Remember El Dedo is a sacred place to them...'

The sick excitement, which had briefly revived Golden Dollar, was now too much for her. She slumped unconscious. The story about the settlers shooting their womenfolk came into my mind again. Then the feeling that the world was turning over returned. I passed my hand over my stubbled face and I could feel my dry leathery tongue protruding past my lips. As I passed out I hoped this would be the last time.

* * *

I became aware of things little by little. The first,

and most important, was that my mouth was wet. Secondly there was something cooling on my skin, taking out the agony caused by three days of frying on the top of El Dedo. From what seemed to be a long way I heard men talking but I could not make out the words.

As I opened my eyes I found that I was in the shade. I seemed to be stretched out on a colourful blanket. Not far away I saw the form of Golden Dollar lying on another. Sitting round us cross-legged were several Apache Indians. Further away the war party was eating a meal of maize.

I sat up, bewildered. This was not the sort of treatment I was expecting at the hands of the Apaches. Then I saw the old man. His face was like creased leather and, like the others, he had the white Apache stripe of war paint across it. Though he was no longer young his body still looked hard and tough.

'Greetings, Bill Tashlin,' he said, coming forward and looking down at me. 'I think our medicine has made you feel better,' he added in fairly good English.

'Greetings, Red Cloud,' I responded. 'We meet under strange circumstances.'

'That is true. The lady is waking. Tell her there is no need for fear.'

Golden Dollar's eyes widened when she saw the circle of Indians about her.

'It's all right,' I said, grabbing her hand. 'We are with friends. This is Chief Red Cloud. He was my father's friend in the old days.'

'Once we were as brothers,' said Red Cloud. 'He taught me your language. I taught him to speak Apache. But now you must eat.'

A brave brought two bowls of steaming maize. At last, when our terrible hunger had abated, I sat cross-legged on my blanket opposite Red Cloud who was puffing peacefully on his pipe. In the distance, by some rocks, I could see what was left of the Noon Gang laid out while some braves scraped shallow graves. I hoped Golden Dollar wouldn't notice their grisly work.

'There are words that must be said,' said Red Cloud after some time. 'I am glad I can speak to the son of Tashlin before I return to the Great Spirit. You know that white men have taken more and more of our land. The herds of buffalo have died because of your hunters. All the time the Indian is driven back. All the time more and more white men come from the East. You are white, but maybe you understand why we make war. It is all there is left for us to do. Only in the desert are we free.'

'I understand you, Red Cloud,' I said. 'But what can one man say? Not all white men are bad, not all Apaches are good.'

Red Cloud inclined his head.

'When I knew your father there was peace, there was still room for both red man and white man. But it changed and I became a warrior. Many were the raiding parties I led.'

'Your fame as a warrior is wide, Red Cloud,' I said.

'Like Geronimo, I am feared,' he continued. 'I am the protector of our tribe. I have no hesitation in killing the invaders. But, son of Tashlin, you must know there was one thing I could not do. I know your father crossed the Gila to search for gold. He never returned, and I know the story told by his partner was that the Apaches had killed him. That was not true. No Apache would have harmed Tashlin. He was my brother.

'When it was told that my braves had killed him, I wept. I knew his partner had made up the lie after he had slain the rest of the party. Yet I was blamed for the murder of my boyhood friend. But now you know the truth. You have found your father's gold, but you have also found the truth. I know too, that the palefaces we killed today were your enemies. Only two have escaped us, but the desert may bring death to them.'

Red Cloud puffed his pipe for a minute.

'I never believed Apaches killed my father,' I said. 'If I had I would not be here today.'

'That is good. Now I shall repay the kindness I owe him. Here is the gold he won from the Gila,' and he pointed to the saddlebags the braves had brought when they carried us down from the summit of El Dedo.

'Take the gold,' Red Cloud continued. 'May it bring you happiness. Now I shall leave you water, I shall leave you food, I shall leave you four horses – the owners no longer need them. When you have rested return to your people. Travel east and you will be safe from attack. Remember Red Cloud has been the true friend of your father. It is written that blood must flow between red man and white man, but some things are more important than war. Friendship is one. I have spoken.'

Red Cloud rose with dignity. At a word his braves leapt astride their horses. The old chief raised his arm in salute. I raised mine. Then the war party cantered off in single file. They were soon lost to sight in the dunes.

'Well,' said Golden Dollar. 'Well...' And there seemed nothing else to say.

CHAPTER 14

'What are you doing there?' asked Golden Dollar, approaching where I stood in the shade of the towering Finger of God, chipping away at its timeworn side.

'Carvin' a name,' I replied. 'Maybe it's sentimental, but it's somethin' I just wanted to do.'

She came over and saw where I was cutting into the red stone the name PABLO MARTINEZ.

'That's a very nice idea,' she said. 'He couldn't have a better monument.'

'Yeah, but a monument won't pat his kids on the head or put an arm round his wife when the nights get lonely.'

It was the day after Red Cloud and his braves had left us. Since their departure we had taken it easy. I think Golden Dollar would have liked to leave the sinister place at once, but after the ordeal on the top of El Dedo de Dios she was too weak to face a journey across the Gila Desert.

I figured with a couple of days rest and plenty of water we'd both be in better shape to start on the way back with our rediscovered gold.

Thinking there was just a slight possibility that Joshua Noon might double back, I made sure the Peacemaker was always handy, though I tried not to let Golden Dollar be aware of this.

But as I chipped at the rock with a heavy knife I was using as a chisel, she said thoughtfully, 'I can't tell you how glad I'll be to get away from here. It may sound crazy, but I keep thinking of Noon and the man who is with him. Supposing they come back...'

'I guess they'll have gone on to where they can get water. He's probably hightailed it to New Jerusalem. Anyways, he'd probably think that the Apaches butchered us with his gang.'

'I hope so,' she muttered with a slight shudder. 'It's strange, but I'll never feel at ease as long as that man is alive. When we leave the Gila, I'd like to head right back East.'

'You can worry about that once we are out of the Gila,' I said. 'Our number one problem is gettin' our gold safely from here to Tombstone.'

'I'm ready to go whenever you like,' she responded. 'This place makes me uneasy. There are ghosts about.'

I nodded in agreement.

Out here, with the Finger dwarfing us and the desert stretching endlessly in every direction, we were no more than a couple of defenceless ants. Even the vast, vivid sky seemed to be crushing down on us.

'I'll cook us a meal an' then we'll start back,' I said, trying to sound cheerful.

Sitting in the shade, under Pablo's name, I soon had a small fire burning and a can of beans cooking. Red Cloud had made sure that we had been given a share of the supplies and water his braves had looted from the Noon Gang's camp.

'Up there, on top of the rock, just after we found the gold...' I began with some difficulty.

Golden Dollar looked me full in the face through the almost invisible smoke of the fire that burned between us. 'I remember,' she said quietly. 'And I think I know what you are going to say. Please don't say it now. I want to get away from the desert first...then, please say it. And please understand.'

'Okay,' I said with a shrug I didn't quite mean. 'You'd be surprised, but I can be an understandin' guy.'

110

Inside I felt disappointment. When you've got a bit of a speech worked out and you're ready to let it go, then you can't help feeling annoyed when you have to hold it back. Then I thought: Maybe it's better if I don't make that speech after all. The desert does funny things to a guy. Maybe back in the world of men I'd wonder how I ever came to put my arms round Golden Dollar in sight of the gold her father robbed from mine!

Anyways, I was getting too old to be sentimental. It would have been easier, too, if I still believed that Golden Dollar was a dancehall tramp, but I knew that – whatever her father had been – at least she was a lady of courage.

So I ladled her some beans, hitched my gunbelt, and said: 'Let's go when we've finished.'

'As soon as you like,' she said with a smile.

I saddled up. We had a mount each, and a packhorse each to lead. These were loaded with the old saddlebags of gold, provisions and waterbags. It was a killing weight, and I knew we wouldn't be able to move much faster than at a walking pace.

I led the way, heading east with El Dedo de Dios gradually shrinking behind us. Only once I turned and looked back at it. It had been well named by the forgotten Spanish explorer. It did look like a giant finger, poised on the edge of the world.

We moved in Indian file, with me picking the best path for the horses. This made it impossible for us to talk properly, and in a way I was relieved about this. After everything that had happened to us there seemed to be nothing to say, and as yet I was not ready to think about spending the treasure.

About mid-afternoon, Golden Dollar suddenly called, 'Look over there.' I turned in my saddle and let my gaze follow her pointing finger. To the north I saw a tiny figure reeling across the desert. Sometimes it would almost disappear from sight as it pitched forward on the sand. Then, with agonising slowness, it would struggle to a kneeling position, painfully get to its feet and plunge a few drunken steps forward before falling again.

'Someone sure looks to be in trouble,' I commented. 'Better see what we can do.' We swung left towards the flopping figure. An old instinct made me unsheath the Peacemaker, and I had it in my hand when we reined up and looked down on the victim of the Gila.

He was a young man with curly hair bleached almost white. His clothes were ragged and torn, and his left trouser leg was black with dried blood. His face was horribly contorted, and the tip of a blackened tongue was starting to protrude from between his split lips. It was the face of a man within an hour of death from thirst.

'Poor thing – how terrible,' murmured Golden Dollar, not realising that we had looked pretty much the same during our last hours on top of the pinnacle.

I slid from my horse and bent over the youth who had now given up the attempt to struggle on. I unscrewed the top of my canteen, poured some water on my kerchief and began to wet his lips. After a couple of minutes his eyes opened. I put the neck of the canteen in his mouth and he began gulping with the rhythm of a mechanical pump.

After several mouthfuls, I eased the canteen away and stood back. It is amazing how the human body responds to water when it needs it. He sat up on the sand and looked at us dumbly, but already life was returning to his face and his eyes were less glazed.

For a minute he stared at Golden Dollar and I, then said in a croaking voice: 'Please, Miss...don't let him kill me.'

'Bill, for God's sake, put your gun away,' she snapped. 'You've scared the poor thing.' She put her arm round his shoulders to reassure him, then began cutting away his left trouser leg to expose a bullet wound in his calf.

'No wonder I scare him,' I said. 'Do you know who he is?'

'Right now I don't care. Come and help me clean this wound. It looks as though he lost a lot of blood.' I knelt down and helped her clean the torn flesh.

'Don't let him kill me,' the youngster muttered deliriously. 'He's Bill Tashlin, Miss...he's a killer...he'll shoot me like a dog...'

'There, there,' said Golden Dollar, wiping his forehead with a wet kerchief.

I was tempted to tell her that this youth had been trying his best to kill us recently, but I could see that his terrible condition had won her womanly sympathy and that a new problem lay ahead.

Maybe if I had had sense I would have given him a bullet, but I could not do it in front of her. Even if you are expected to be at ease killing, it is pretty hard to look at the face of a dying man down a gun barrel.

'We must make camp and I'll nurse him,' said Golden Dollar. 'Then, when he's a bit better, he can travel back with us. He's the one who escaped from the Indian attack with Joshua Noon, isn't he?'

'Yep,' I agreed. 'His name is Valentine Love, he's about nineteen or twenty, an' I've heard tell he's related to Joshua Noon. He's been one of his hangers-on for some time.'

'Well, whatever his past, we couldn't leave him here to die,' she said. So while she tended the blond boy, I made camp.

For a few hours his mind wandered, but by evening he had recovered a lot and was able to speak more clearly after Golden Dollar had fed him some soup.

'Thanks, Miss, you are an angel,' he whispered. 'But please don't let him...' he nodded to me. 'Don't let him...'

'Don't worry now. He'll not hurt you.' She turned to me. 'Why is he so afraid you'll harm him?'

'Because he knows that's what he or Noon would have done to me if it had been the other way round,' I said.

She turned away, looking disappointed with my cynical reply. I could not help feeling that she was almost siding with the young outlaw against me. But, as I've said, the desert does funny things to people and everything gets kind of crazy at times. Maybe I was feeling this way because Val Love was something that I could have done without.

'What happened to Joshua Noon?' I asked him.

'Goddam him to hell,' he muttered, his face a sudden grimace of hate. 'He led me into all this, and then he does this to me....'

'What did he do?'

Val Love told us how he had fled with Joshua Noon from El Dedo de Dios with a bunch of braves after them. This was when an Apache bullet went through his leg. Somehow they had managed to shake off the Indians, but they found that Noon's horse had also stopped a bullet. When it finally plunged onto the sand, Noon had shared Val's mount.

They made camp when they felt they were safe, but in the morning when the young man woke he found that Joshua Noon had taken his horse and deserted him.

'He left me to die of thirst,' he said in a sobbing voice. 'He'd been like a Pa to me, but when the chips were down he rode off while I was asleep. An' I didn't have no one else in the world but him.'

'Did he teach you to shoot?' I asked.

He nodded. 'He taught me everythin' after my folks passed on. I was in his gang an' I'd have given my life for him.. .an' yet he just rode off!'

'You expect something different from a coyote?' I

asked, disgusted with the tears that were welling from his eyes.

'How dare you talk to him like that?' demanded Golden Dollar. 'Can't you understand   how he feels. You should – you were also a gunslinger at his age, remember!
'

'Sorry,' I said. 'I was forgetting. I just can't forget that three days ago he was lookin' at us over a rifle sight.'

'Things have changed since then. He deserves a second chance after what he has been through.'

'I guess you could be right,' I agreed finally.

* * *

At sun up we continued our journey. I walked, and Val Love, who had improved a lot, rode my horse beside Golden Dollar. The pack animals toiled behind them.

As the morning wore on, the young man's spirits seemed to rise. He seemed to have things to say that amused Golden Dollar. I was not so amused, but maybe I felt some sort of jealousy. Though he was still worn-looking, he was a pretty handsome boy, with his ragged white hair round his bronzed face and his slim, narrow-hipped body hinting of lithe power. Maybe I felt put out because he happened to be nearly ten years younger.

'How did you get away from the Apaches, Miss?' he asked. Golden Dollar told him about Red Cloud.

'So you found the gold after all,' he mused.

'Yes,' she answered. 'It's in those saddlebags.'

'I only hope your friend gives you your fair share,' he said in a low voice.

I pretended not to hear.

The desert was beginning to change. It was not quite so harsh. Here and there a cactus gave a hint of something alive. Sometimes the hot wind drove tumbleweed towards us. Idly I wondered how many miles they had come, and I wondered how long it would be before we escaped the ill-omened Gila.

CHAPTER 15

The eye-straining blue of the desert sky had paled and the sun was drowning in blood behind us when we camped for the night. I tethered the animals while Val Love helped Golden Dollar light a small bundle of firewood to prepare the evening beans and coffee.

As we sat round the small fire, Val said abruptly, 'Mr Tashlin, I guess I'd like you to know just how much I 'predate what you an' this lady have done for me. I owe my life to you, an' I guess there ain't no reason in the world why you shouldn't have left me for the buzzards...'

'I guess that's what you expected me to do,' I grinned.

'I guess so, considerin' everythin' that's happened,' he admitted, looking at the glowing embers. 'Anyways, I feel a hell of a lot better today. Maybe tomorrow I can walk a bit.'

'Not on that leg,' I said. 'You don't wanna open the wound again.'

As I saw his young face reflected in the firelight, with the background of purpling sky, I realised I had lost the dislike I'd felt for him.

It suddenly did not matter any more that earlier on he would have killed me if he'd had the chance. He'd been on one side – I had been on the other. He had been Joshua Noon's man, and, rightly or wrongly, I was the enemy. Even more, I realised, as I saw him sitting there beside Golden Dollar, that it was like looking back on my own youth.

I had been forced to use a gun, so how could I

judge him when he'd learnt the facts of life from Joshua Noon. He was still a kid really, and maybe in saving him I was in some way making up for that kid I had shot in Las Cruces.

'What'll you do when you get back?' Golden Dollar asked him.

'I guess I'll look up Uncle Joshua,' he said grimly. 'There's a reckoning comin' to him.'

'If you're smart, you'll forget him,' I said. 'There's been enough bloodlettin' already. Maybe I'm gonna get a ranch for myself. There'd be a job on it for you if you were interested...'

'That's a fine thing for you to offer,' he said.

By now the stars were out and a breeze blew gently across the face of the cooling desert.

'Guess we'd better get some sleep,' I said. 'We should hit the Tombstone trail with a bit of luck tomorrow.'

'Say, Mr Tashlin, if you wanna rope me up I wouldn't mind. I mean – why should you trust me, an' with all that gold in the bags, you might sleep easier.'

'What a crazy thing to say,' said Golden Dollar. 'We trust you.'

'Thanks for your kindness, Miss,' he said as we rolled up in our blankets. 'I hope I can repay it someday.'

* * *

Another day dawned. Another day of thirst and weariness to be got through somehow. I helped Val Love into my saddle and felt the waterbags. They were far too light.

I was adjusting the load on one of the pack animals when Golden Dollar walked over to me.

'Bill, there's something I want to tell you,' she said quietly, throwing an uneasy glance to where Val Love was sitting unconcernedly on my horse.

'Say on,' I said, pulling the girth strap extra tight

117

because the animals were rapidly becoming just skin and bone with the desert conditions.

'Last night.. .when you were asleep...Val Love came over to me...and he tried...'

I laughed. 'That doesn't really shock me,' I said. 'You're still a pretty girl even after the heat of the Gila. He didn't get rough, did he?'

'Oh no...he was quite sweet really, and went away when I told him I wasn't interested,' she said thoughtfully. 'He just smiled and said there was plenty of time.'

'I guess he figures I'm too old an' weather-beaten to be in the runnin',' I grinned, but I wasn't exactly grinning inside.

'Well, I just thought I'd mention it,' she said.

'Thanks a lot,' I said. 'I hope you've satisfied your female vanity by passin' on that information. Now let's get crackin'.'

'You silly fool,' snapped Golden Dollar going a shade of red under her tan. Without a word she swung herself into her saddle. I grabbed the halter of a packhorse and began to lead the way east.

Ahead the desert danced. Behind Golden Dollar seemed to forget whatever had happened during the night. Soon she was laughing at Val Love's remarks. To amuse her he began to sing in a pleasant voice *The Outlaw's Lament*. It was a song with the same tune as *The Streets of Laredo*.

> '*O, I am a young outlaw way down from Wyoming,*
> *I live by my six-gun, and the gold it brings me.*
> *I hold up the stage coach, and I hold up the freight train,*
> *I have a fine life – and my gun makes me free!*
>
> '*O, in the card houses you often will find me*
> *With a price on my head and gold for my fee.*
> *And though I am wanted, no one will dare harm me*
> *For I'm quick on the draw – and my gun keeps me free!*

'O, I roam o'er the West from Nevada to Texas,
And I love a young girl who only loves me.
Her name is Dolores and she lives cross the border,
And so I won't lose her my gun works for me!

'O, tonight I am going to meet my Dolores.
There's a light in her window that's just meant for me,
I'll whistle our love song and her lips will be waiting...
And I have no fear 'cause my gun keeps me free!

'O, I'm under her window, "Come down, dear Dolores!"
Then a shot from her doorway is aimed straight at me.
I feel my life ebbing while the sheriff is laughing –
And I can't raise my pistol and I can't even see!

'O, I was a young outlaw way down from Wyoming,
But no more with my gun will I ride bold and free,
For the girl that I loved had no use for an outlaw
But only the dollars that were offered for me...'

The sun climbed higher. Under its rays I often felt giddy as I trudged alone at the head of our small party. The swishing of our tiny water supply in the waterbags seemed to add to my thirst, but it was so low I dared not drink until it was absolutely necessary.

Sometimes I stumbled over rocks, and more and more thorn bushes tore at the legs of my Levi's – an indication that we were leaving the arid desert behind. Here and there a greasewood tree gave a little pool of shade and clumps of chaparral had become more common.

About noon I halted to rest and water the horses. Golden Dollar dismounted to get water for Val Love. I was just about to drink from my canteen when I heard the click of a safety catch and the voice of Val Love saying: 'Drop that, Tashlin. Raise your hands an' turn round, or you'll be ventilated.'

I obeyed. The canteen thumped the sand and a dark snake of water spread from its neck. A pity about that

119

water! Turning slowly with my hands at shoulder level, I saw that he had my rifle in his hands and its round cold eye was pointing steadily at my stomach.

'I guess you was a bit careless to leave your Winchester in its scabbard,' he laughed.

'I guess I trusted you,' I said with a shrug.

He laughed again.

'We all make mistakes, even you, Tashlin. You Miss, undo his gunbelt buckle and let his gun drop. Any funny stuff an' you'll both find yourselves dead.'

'Do as he says,' I told Golden Dollar. 'He's of the killer breed and our lives mean nothin' to him.'

'You're dead right there, Tashlin,' he said. 'I'd snuff you out just as I'd squash a fly. But the lady is a different matter at the moment. We have some unfinished business.'

With a look of disbelief on her face, Golden Dollar undid the silver buckle that held my belt. It slid over my hips and came to rest in a circle of leather and cartridges at my feet. I stepped out of it and moved back.

'Now what?' I asked, my hands still up.

'You can both sit down over there,' he said, indicating the spot with his rifle barrel. We did as he said. Then he carefully slid down from the horse, limped over and picked up my gunbelt with one hand and hung it on the saddle horn of my horse.

'Why are you doing this after we saved you?' demanded Golden Dollar, tears of rage in her eyes. 'We could have left you to die.'

'Sure you could have, Miss, an' you'd have been a damn sight smarter if you had. Lemme tell you one thing – there is one rule in the desert an' that is that you must look after yourself. Joshua Noon did that when he left me. Now, I'm gonna do the same, only I'll come out with enough of the yellow stuff to make me rich for life.'

'Listen,' I said. 'I can understand how you want the

gold like anyone else would, but there ain't no need for this. What say we split it three ways an' call it quits...'

'You can't get round me, Tashlin,' he said softly as he climbed painfully back into the saddle. 'You only talk of sharing the gold because you have a yellow streak instead of a spine.'

'What are you going to do, then?' asked Golden Dollar.

'Nothing yet, Miss. We'll carry on until we reach the trail, then we'll leave Mr Tashlin an' you an' I will go on a bit of the way together. If you come to think about it, we could have some fun especially with all that gold to spend. After all, Miss, you'd be better with me than Tashlin. He'd do you out of your share. What you need is a young buck like me who can really appreciate you...'

'Never,' she snapped.

'I like a bit of spirit in my women,' he drawled. 'But as long as I got this gun, Miss, I'll be able to do what I like. Hear that, Tashlin, I got your gold an' your woman.'

Val Love seemed to have the upper hand. I could only sit there and wait to see what happened.

'Now, we'll get movin',' he said. 'You lead the way, Tashlin. Miss, you can ride your pony and lead the pack hosses. I'll follow behind. Any tricks an' I'll let you have a bullet apiece.. .an' you might remember I was the best rifle shot in the Noon bunch.'

Without a word I got to my feet and once more began to march across the desert.

'Go straight, Tashlin,' called Val Love. 'Don't get no fancy notions about leadin' us away from the trail. You take us to the trail an' I'll leave you there with some water an' you'll have a chance, but any tricks an' you'll be buzzard-meat.'

He was in a good mood, which was no wonder with the thousands of dollars worth of gold in his grasp.

He even burst into snatches of song:

> *'O, I am a young outlaw way down from Wyoming,*
> *I live by my six-gun, and the gold it brings me.*
> *I hold up the stage coach, and I hold up the freight*
>   *train,*
> *I have a fine life – and my gun makes me free!'*

An hour later I stopped on top of a rise. To the east I could see a faint trail cut across the desert face. Golden Dollar reined up.

'There it is,' I said. 'We're out of the Gila.'

Thanks a lot, Tashlin,' called Val Love. 'Just turn round willya...'

I turned slowly with the knowledge of what was going to happen.

Sitting on his horse, he had the rifle raised and was grinning down the barrel at me. I guess he had made me turn because he wanted to see the expression on my face when he pulled the trigger.

'No! No!' screamed Golden Dollar.

Val Love pulled the trigger, but there was only a click. He looked so surprised his face was almost funny. I dived forward. It seemed an eternity as my footsteps sank into the sand, and I had the feeling you get in those dreams when you're running away from Indians yet hardly move at all.

Then I was beside his horse. I grabbed his wounded leg and pulled with all my strength. He gave a yelp of agony and struggled to keep in the saddle. The horse whinnied and reared, and Val Love came tumbling down over its haunches.

I backed away from the hooves of the plunging animal while Val Love climbed unsteadily to his feet.

'You ain't won yet, Tashlin,' he snarled.

'Wanna bet,' I replied, and rushed him.

I dropped my head low and butted him in the belly, at the same time throwing my arms round his waist. He grunted. Stars whirled through my brain as he brought his locked fists down on the back of my neck. But my charge carried him before me and a second later we were sprawling in a heap.

He tried to get his hands round my throat, but, though my head was still reeling, I managed to get clear and roll away from his reach. He got to his feet again and, with his good leg, swung a kick that caught me painfully on the jaw. It threw him off balance and his injured leg crumpled under him.

Val Love was a tough young hombre. He was on his knees in an instant, a big rock held in his hands. Dazed with the blows to my head, I tried to move out of range. He hurled it with all his strength and it crashed into my left shoulder. Without giving him time to grab another, I launched myself at him though I could only see a blurred outline through the curtain of pain before my eyes.

Again we tangled, punching, kicking and cursing each other to hell. At one time he was astride my chest, at another I was atop him and with my hands round his throat, trying to choke the life out of him.

The next thing I remember was a blow on the right temple. For a moment I was stunned. Val Love hopped to his feet and left me. If this had been an ordinary grudge fight he would have followed his advantage and hit me again. But this was a fight to the death.

For a moment I lay on the sand with the world and sky spinning about me. I was dimly aware that Val Love had limped to his horse where the Peacemaker hung in its holster from the saddle horn.

With a wolfish grin of triumph on his battered young features he grasped the gun by its butt.

'Goddam you, Tashlin, this is where you really get it,' he cried.

I could see his leg was troubling him. Even as he tried to aim at me he staggered. Summoning every ounce of strength I had left, I leapt at him. He was a good target, being silhouetted on the edge of the rise against the brilliant sky.

I crashed into him before he could fire. He reeled backwards, the Peacemaker waving wildly in his hand. Then he was rolling over and over down the slope. I stood on the edge and watched him reach the bottom where he came to rest against a large black rock.

As my eyes focused, I saw there was something coiled and gleaming in the sun on top of it. Then I heard the whirring sound that instantly makes your blood as cold as the water of a snowy mountain stream. The sun-basking rattlesnake poised to strike.

I saw Val Love raise the sixgun to aim at the swaying head. Then came a click. He had not realised that I had removed the cartridges from the chambers of the Colt just as I had unloaded the Winchester while he slept.

I had given the young desperado his chance, but I had also taken precautions against his killer instinct.

'For God's sake, help me, Tashlin,' he implored. There was a series of clicks as the cylinder of the revolver turned uselessly. Then the snake struck.

Val Love gave one scream and began to die.

CHAPTER 16

White-faced, Golden Dollar came forward to say something.

'There's nothing to say,' I said. 'We all make mistakes about people – and gold fever is the worst disease in the world.'

I turned and began climbing down the slope. By the time I reached the sprawled form of the late Valentine Love, the rattler had departed. I picked up the Peacemaker and scrambled back. Here I took cartridges from my belt and loaded the Colt and then the Winchester.

'I really believed there was a chance for him,' said Golden Dollar, her eyes close to tears, as we mounted our horses.

'I know,' I said, 'but, though he was only a kid, he had killer's eyes which is why, I guess, I unloaded the weapons.'

For the rest of the day we followed the trail and made camp at sunset. Early next morning our track joined the main Tucson-Tombstone trail.

'From what I remember, we should hit the town about noon,' I said. 'The first thing to do will be get the gold deposited in the bank, then get cleaned up. An' you must have the doc look at that wound in your arm.'

She nodded.

'You look terrible, but I'm sure I must look even worse.'

'You look pretty ragged,' I grinned. 'But at least the desert sun has made your hair even more like real gold.'

'A pretty speech, Mr Tashlin,' she smiled. 'Well, in a few days I expect it will be back to the old life...'

'I guess we should have a little talk about that,' I said. 'Earlier on you said you didn't want to talk about things until we were out of the Gila. Well, we are now, an' what I suggest is this—we found the gold together so we should split it fifty-fifty. Apart from what we send to Pablo's wife.'

It seemed a slight frown crossed her face. 'I didn't realise it was about that you wished to speak at El Dedo de Dios,' she said. 'Anyway, you know the truth about my father and yours. Surely you don't want to share with the daughter of the man who...'

'Forget it,' I said. 'The past is the past. Once our gold is in the bank I'm gonna hang up my gun. I've had enough of being a gunfighter, of always bein' alone because I'm quick on the draw, of bein' regarded as some sort of murder machine. That life is over. Instead I'm gonna buy a ranch somewhere peaceful...'

I paused. Now came the difficult part. I had never asked anyone to marry me before.

'There was somethin' else I was thinkin' of mentionin' at El Dedo de Dios,' I said. 'I'd be mighty glad if you'd share the ranch with me as well as the gold. On the strict understandin' you'd be Mrs Tashlin. Let's both make a new start together.' She turned a cool look on me.

'You really want to marry me?'

'That' s the general idea.'

'Bill, I'm a dancehall girl. I'm the daughter of your father's killer. Several times in the past, when you've been mad at me, you've said "Like father, like daughter." I don't want to live with a man who throws that up in my face when he gets sore. I appreciate you sharing the gold with me...but this is kind of different. I can't see myself fitting into the kind of life you're planning.'

'The hell with it,' I said. 'I promise I'll never

mention your father, or the past, or anything. There's been enough hate. Let's forget it. Just remember my promise.'

'In that case, Bill Tashlin, I accept your proposal. I shall try and make you a good wife.'

I guess in romance stories when this stage is reached the folk concerned immediately kiss and say a lot of sweet nothings to each other. But we didn't. We just rode on. There was no need to prove anything. All that had been done out on the Gila.

'Now, I've got something to tell you,' she said. 'Seeing I'm going to be Mrs Tashlin I'm telling you, otherwise, because you're a cussed guy, I was going to be cussed, too, and never say a word.'

'Speak on,' I said cheerfully.

'I know how you felt about your father...'

I raised my hand. 'I thought we weren't going to mention the past.'

'Just this once we are. I guess you love me all right, Bill Tashlin. But deep down you'd never be quite at ease. When we have our children you'd think that one of their grandfathers murdered the other. It'd be an odd situation... Maybe you'd fear the killer strain would be inherited. Sure, you wouldn't say anything but you wouldn't be a natural man if you didn't think along those lines. So let me tell you the true story. My mother was widowed when I was quite small. She got married again to a man called Sherman, but it never worked out. My stepfather treated her bad, and I never knew life could be so unhappy. Yet, in a strange way, I think he loved her. It was as though there was a devil inside him he could not control. Finally he left. He went back to the West.'

'You mean...Sherman was your stepfather?'

'Yes. I guess when he was dying he felt some sort of remorse. That is why he sent me that letter. In some way he wanted to put things right.'

I felt a boulder had been rolled off my heart.

'Why the hell didn't you tell me before?' I demanded angrily.

'I didn't think you would believe me. You wouldn't have, and I didn't like you well enough then,' she laughed. 'You've got some irritating ways.'

We rode on. A couple of hours later we were overtaken by the Wells Fargo stage. As it swayed past the driver and the shotgun looked at us pretty hard, but they didn't stop.

At last we were passing Boothill on our left. Next minute we saw a tubby figure coming down the trail towards us on a mule. Even at a distance I had no difficulty in recognising it.

'It's our friend from the Press,' I said. 'Milton Homer, coming hotfoot to get the story I promised him.'

'Howdy,' greeted Milton breathlessly when we met.

Before I could reply, he rattled on, 'I've got to warn you, Joshua Noon is back in town. He'll know you're heading this way because the stage driver has spread the word. Turn round while you can. That man is in a real mean mood.'

'Let's go, Bill,' said Golden Dollar. 'Having come so far I don't want to risk losing you now.'

'She's right, Mr Tashlin,' chimed in Milton. 'He's out for revenge. I'll come part of the way with you...' He tugged out his big notebook. 'Maybe you can give me the details of your adventures as we go along together.'

'Stick around, you'll get a story firsthand,' I said curtly. 'We're going on.'

'But, Bill, why?' asked Golden Dollar.

'Because, as Red Cloud might say, it is written. If we run now we'll always be in fear. At the back of our minds will be the thought that someday, somewhere Joshua Noon might turn up. It would be poison. You wait here. I'm going to settle it now.'

She shook her head and produced her little Derringer.

'I'm coming with you. You'll need someone to guard the gold while... while...' Her words trailed off and we rode on in silence.

Milton Homer was sweating. No doubt he was excited at the prospect of a story, but he was also a bit nervous being so close to us. Any minute now the lead would start to fly.

As we approached the straggling outskirts of the town I saw a youth take one look at me, then race down the street. Obviously he was a lookout.

The streets were strangely deserted. A tumbleweed blew down Allen Street towards me. Then I noticed the eyes... eyes that looked from behind curtains, eyes that looked from chinks in walls, eyes that squinted at us over fences.

We halted by the OK Corral and tethered the horses to the rail opposite the saddle shop.

'Keep out of the way,' I said to Golden Dollar.

She was about to come over to my side, but Milton took her by the arm and hurried her away from me.

'Be careful... darling,' she said.

I nodded. She need have no fear of me not being careful. Having been so close to death the last few days, I had no desire to improve the acquaintanceship.

Stiffly I began to walk down Allen Street to where it was crossed by 4th Street. I was half-way between the OK Corral and the Can Can Restaurant when the bat-wing doors of the Crystal Palace Saloon flapped open. Joshua Noon strolled out.

Immediately I forgot the hidden spectators. I forgot the woman who said she would be my wife. I forgot the gold still loaded on the packhorses. My entire concentration was fixed on this black clad gunman.

I stopped, my right hand swinging close to the butt

129

of the Peacemaker.

Noon did not say a word. His hand streaked down to his holster and reappeared with his gun. He fired from the hip, a method giving speed rather than accuracy. In gunfighting the trick is to manage to hold your fire until you have the gun high enough to get a good sight on your enemy.

His first bullet went wide. My gun crashed a second after his. I had my sights on his head, but he ducked away and a window of the saloon shattered behind him. He fired again, and the bullet ripped away half the lobe of my left ear. I could feel the warm flow down my neck.

Noon threw himself into a doorway and began firing round the jamb. I was unprotected in the street, so I ran into the porch of the Allen Bank on the other side. A bullet kicked up dust beside me as I just managed to get behind cover. But I was in a bad position. Unless I was going to risk exposing myself, I would have to fire with my left hand. Rather than waste ammunition, I decided to let Noon make the next move.

I did not have to wait long. He darted into the open to try and get me. A slug splintered the woodwork close to my belly. I dropped on my knee and sent one back.

Noon dodged behind a cart loaded with bales of straw. Underneath it I could see his legs plainly and I tried to shoot them. Realising he was without cover below the waist, he suddenly dived into Bob Hatch's Billiard Hall. Afraid he might get out through a back door, I took a chance and ran across the street after him.

A bullet caught me in the thigh and I went over like a skittle. From somewhere I heard Golden Dollar's scream. I raised myself on my left hand and aimed the Colt with the right at the door of the Billiard Hall, waiting for Noon to return to finish me off.

Seconds passed. My thigh felt as though a red hot

iron had been passed through it. Luckily the bone had not been shattered.

Then Joshua Noon appeared at the door. I realised he must have been reloading behind it. We were only a few yards apart. He grinned as he saw me sprawled in the street. Then our guns went off almost together...almost but not quite. My bullet got home first and its impact shook him so that his shot went wide. I caught a glimpse of crimson on his shirt, before he reeled back out of sight.

I hauled myself to my feet and began to drag my way to the Billiard Hall, leaving a trail of blood in the street.

The door had swung shut, and I had to push it open with my free hand. Inside the place seemed to be empty. I guessed the customers must have fled out the back exit when they saw the battle was heading in their direction.

There were several billiard tables in a row. Some still had balls on them. There was no sign of Noon. Cautiously I advanced. Suddenly there was an echoing crash of a revolver. I felt a second burning pain, this time in my right arm. My fingers refused to obey me and the Peacemaker fell to the floor.

Noon had risen up from behind the far billiard table. He stood, supporting himself with his left hand on the table while he raised the gun to end the combat.

I threw myself forward just in time. The bullet threw up splinters somewhere behind me. With my left hand I groped for my gun.

I got it and raised it shakily. Noon was swaying badly. His breath made a horrible rasping sound. For a second we looked each other in the face... Then, just as I pulled the trigger, his gun dropped. I think he was dead when my second bullet struck him.

He sprawled forward across the billiard table. A white ball rolled away from him and a little crimson serpent began to creep over the green baize.

131

Behind me the door flew open and Golden Dollar ran in. Seeing me covered in blood she came and put her arm round me. Painfully, I limped out of the Billiard Hall.

Outside a crowd was gathering. Several people were peering through the windows at the still form inside. No one spoke.

'Someone get a doctor, he's bleeding bad,' cried Golden Dollar. Milton Homer ran off.

'I'll be all right,' I muttered.

With great effort, I raised the Colt Peacemaker .45 in my left hand. I looked at it closely and thought about the years I had worn it on my thigh. I remembered the hours I had practised with it. I remembered the battles I had fought, and the times it had saved my life. It had been my pride and protector and then I wondered about the men I had killed with it.

With Golden Dollar supporting me, I managed to stagger to a nearby well. Here I threw my ghun into the shaft to vanish into its muddy depths. My career as a gun-slinger was ended.